*Things
Kept,
Things
Left
Behind*

The

Iowa

Short

Fiction

Award

University of

Iowa Press

Iowa City

~~Jim Tomlinson~~ *Jim Tomlinson* Nov 3, 2008

Things
Kept,
Things
Left Behind

University of Iowa Press, Iowa City 52242

Copyright © 2006 by Jim Tomlinson

http://www.uiowa.edu/uiowapress

The publication of this book was generously supported by
the National Endowment for the Arts.

The University of Iowa Press is a member of Green Press
Initiative and is committed to preserving natural resources.
Printed on acid-free paper

Library of Congress Cataloging-in-Publication Data
Tomlinson, Jim, 1941–.
     Things kept, things left behind / Jim Tomlinson.
        p.   cm.—(The Iowa short fiction award)
     Contents: First husband, first wife—Lake Charles—The
accomplished son—Squirrels—Things kept—Paragon tea—
Flights—Things left behind—Marathon man—Prologue
(two lives in letters)—Stainless.
     ISBN 0-87745-991-6 (pbk.)
     I. Title.   II. Series.   TOML
PS3620.O575T47 2006
813'.6—dc22   2006041803

06 07 08 09 10 P 5 4 3 2 1

For Gin Petty

Like the litter of lost coal shining
in moonlight, this is the place

we come to when decisions need to be
made. Each time we are drawn

to this spot, a strip of bright metal
at the edge of the rail.

—RON HOUCHIN, "Crossties"

Contents

ACKNOWLEDGMENTS

I would like to thank the editors of the publications in which
these stories have appeared: "First Husband, First Wife," *Five
Points* (September 2006); "Stainless," *The Pinch* (Spring 2006);
"Squirrels," *Duck and Herring PFG* (Fall 2005); "Paragon Tea,"
WIND, A Journal of Writing and Community (July 2005);
"Flights," *SmokeLong Quarterly* (December 2005) and
SmokeLong Annual 2006 (Fall 2006); and "Marathon Man,"
Grand Prize Winner, Nougat Magazine's Annual Fiction
Contest, *Nougat* (September 2005).

    I wish to express my heartfelt thanks to the House Writers
—Beth, Cynthia, Barbara, Shelda, Steve, and Jean—for their
insights, encouragement, and friendship; to the Kentucky Arts
Council for its generous financial support; to the donors, sup-
porters, and staff of the Carnegie Center for Literacy and Learn-
ing in Lexington, Kentucky, for keeping the doors open; and to
Mike, Lee, George Ella, Leatha, Silas, Chris, Ron, and everyone
else at the Hindman Settlement School's Appalachian Writers
Workshop, where writing becomes a joyous and inspiring thing.
For their generous spirit and sage advice, sincere thanks also go
to the good folks at the Sewanee Writers' Conference—Wyatt
Prunty and Cheri Peters, Richard Bausch, Jill McCorkle, Tony
Earley, the full faculty, staff, fellows, scholars, and contributors all.

    And always, a special thanks to Gin Petty.

First
Husband,
First
Wife

It was Jerry Cole's ex-wife, Cheryl, who lifted the drugs, which were already illegal anyway. She boosted them from this fat pill lady who manages Hilltop Green Assisted Living. As Jerry waited outside behind the wheel of his rust-bucket GMC piece-of-crap pickup truck parked at the curb, as he sat there imagining how good things would be now that his luck was finally changing, Cheryl's chrome beautician cart came careening down Hilltop Green's front walk like a runaway Peterbilt. Cheryl herself followed close behind, the shoebox stash tucked under her arm for anyone with eyes to see.

She handed the box through the window, stowed the cart in back, and climbed in. Three times she slammed the door, harder each time, until finally it latched. Her face was all wadded up with stupid worry, was it right or was it wrong, this thing they were doing. He lifted the lid and grabbed three bottles out, read the labels, then pushed them close to her face. See? He said, pointing to the people's names, the dates. Isn't it just like I told you? They're dead, aren't they, long ago dead, if they were ever alive, if they aren't someone's made-up names.

Cheryl's eyes got teary. Okay, she said, okay. He said, There's no way Fat-Ass reports this stuff missing. You just relax, babe. Her fists burrowed into her lap. Okay, she said again, and she wiped her cheek on his shoulder. Don't be like that, he said. She said, I'll try, Jerry, really I will.

While he drove, Cheryl pawed through the jumble. She picked out bottles, shaking each one like a baby's rattle. She read labels out loud to him, sounding out the syllables of the chemical names. Jesus, she said, I don't recognize none of this stuff.

No problem, Jerry said, feeling juiced now that they were on the interstate. We'll get us a D.A.R.E. book, he said, sort it all out, what we can sell, what to flush.

Jerry, she yelled. Slow down! He was changing lanes, passing cars on both sides. The pickup vibrated, shuddered, the steering wheel numbing his hands. The speedometer needle was waggling a blur around eighty. He backed off the gas, downshifted, and dropped back to legal speed.

He'd had to let Cheryl do the actual swiping, even though she wasn't cut out for it. She worked at Hilltop Green, came and went all the time, fixing old people's hair in their rooms. She had natural access, which Jerry considered important for successful burglary. That's also how, in the first place, she came to be poking around the manager's room, how she happened upon that shoebox hidden high on a closet shelf. Cheryl had always been the kind of person who liked to look at other people's stuff. She'd open drawers and touch a few things, maybe try on shoes or jewelry, check out what's in the medicine cabinet, dab ointment, maybe sniff some perfume. That's all, though. Jacking those pills would never cross her mind, not in a million years. Jerry had to help her see that shoebox for the opportunity it was.

Even though she was the one who took the pill lady's stash, Jerry was the one who got caught. It happened when he tried to broker the Lorcet. His buyer, this muscle-bound freak with a bullet-shaped head and a dragon tattoo glommed onto his jugular, turned out to be a cop, his killer tattoo a fake. A Lexington TV reporter called Jerry a regional drug lord. A station cameraman shot video of him in his orange jail jumpsuit, leg-chains dragging as he waddled up the courthouse steps. The station ran the tape on the newscasts at six and eleven. Cheryl rented a VCR, and she tried to record it so he could see. The piece-of-crap machine screwed up, though, taping some revivalist preacher instead, a completely different channel.

While Cheryl's trial got delayed and delayed, Jerry got convicted and served eight months at Blackburn Correctional Facility. It felt like eight years. The day he was to get out was also his thirtieth birthday, which he took to be some kind of sign. When he woke up that last prison morning, his mind was filled with thoughts of change, of setting off in new directions. He thought maybe he'd start an herb farm on five acres his cousin Shuey owned. Or he'd fence those acres and raise emus, raise them for meat, sell it to restaurants. Or maybe he'd get into ginseng, what Shuey called "sang." The stuff grew wild in Daniel Boone National Forest, old stuff, premium stuff. Foreigners paid small fortunes for a wild-grown root shaped like an animal, a duck, a horse, or maybe a hog. Sang just grew out there, grew in plain dirt, knuckles of the stuff like shallow nuggets of gold, a waiting fortune for someone with ambition to find it. As he lay on his bunk, Jerry could almost feel it in his fingers, smell the soft, musty earth as it crumbled away to reveal the root's shape. His wasted months at Blackburn were ending today. His life was starting again. This time he'd get it right.

Cheryl had rented a motel room not two miles from Blackburn's main gate. She'd decorated it with yellow balloons and rainbow streamers. She bought the fancy Kroger cheese-and-cold-cut platter and laid it out on one bed, a washtub of ice and beer stationed at the foot. She even baked his favorite strawberry jam cake. Two blocky number candles were stuck in the coconut frosting, a three and a zero. As soon as they got to the room, Cheryl lit the candles, shut the drapes, and switched off the lights. She started singing a birthday song, the one the Beatles sang, while performing a cheerleader-style dance in the flickery light. As she did, Jerry inched over to the beer tub. Kneeling there, he uncapped his first bottle since forever, brought its cold lips to his, and pointed the bottom to the swirly motel ceiling. His mind started thinking about riverboats on the Ohio. Did they run in winter when the weather got too cold to dig sang? He wondered about their casinos, what they looked for in card dealers, if a felony conviction would hurt someone's chances.

Where are you? Cheryl asked, her face near his, the smell of her bubblegum everywhere. She was still breathing hard from the dancing, but the song was over. Who? Jerry asked. Where? He looked behind him, lifted a bedspread corner, stood and looked all around as though someone else might be there. He lurched toward Cheryl and poked a hand at her ribs. She dodged, squealing, her elbows tucked for protection. He said, That really was great, babe, just great, the song. He grabbed an armload of her then and wrestled her onto the bed. He pinned her there, blowing mouth-farts across her soft, surging belly. A taste like herbs was slick on his lips and tongue. Changing his life, he decided, could wait one more day.

The candles melted down. Their flames grew wide and flickered and blistered the frosting. A sugar char smell filled the room, sweet like campfire marshmallows. Jerry rolled off the bed and blew out the blaze. As he lay back down, he said, Marry me. I did, she said. Haven't we had this talk, Jerry, maybe eighty-nine times? Monkeylike, he scrambled across her. Then marry me *again*. He said it as if it were something totally new. Never, she said. His lip pouted out, and he made a whimpering sound. She combed his hair with her fingers and kissed his neck. You'll always be my first husband, she said.

They were kids when they married. Later, Jerry had another wife, six months, that one a real mistake. She's somewhere in Iowa now, she and the twins. After Jerry, Cheryl had two husbands, the last one, Fenton, a real bastard. One night a couple years into that marriage, she called Jerry's house, waking him, her words all mush-mouthed. Fenton, the son of a bitch, had been beating on her for no good reason, threatening her, sticking the barrel of his fancy pistol in her mouth like it was his dick. Jerry got there fast. He caught the guy scrambling out the back door, got his gun away, and creased his skull with it. With his bare fists he busted up

Fenton's face. Cheryl packed up what was rightfully hers, and they loaded it all into Jerry's pickup. They left Fenton on the kitchen linoleum, unconscious and bleeding a puddle. Jerry drove her back to his place and unloaded her stuff into the bedroom that used to be theirs.

Cheryl calls herself a three-time loser when it comes to marriage, says it with a quick smile whenever talk heads that direction. She doesn't mean it, though, not really. It's instinctive, like turning with a punch to take away some of its sting.

Jerry's better than most about hitting her. He rarely does, and then it's because of some incredibly stupid, unthinking thing she's done. And it's never with fists. Never. That's nothing compared to the good things he's done, like getting her away from Fenton. One time he gave her this absolutely perfect making-up present, a calico kitten that she named Myrtle. And now, his refusing to finger her about the drugs, even when they offered probation if he'd just testify against her. Cheryl doesn't know what love feels like, not for sure. Her history is too messy for certainty about that. But on his best days Jerry does the sweetest things anyone's ever done for her. She likes how it makes her feel, and she thinks maybe that feeling is love.

She puts her spiral notebook in her purse for her meeting with Suggs, the lawyer assigned by the court. Usually they meet in his courthouse office, which he shares with four other public defenders. She thinks of it as an office of stalls—milking stalls, toilet stalls, small stalls, hardly room for someone to yawn. On the phone, Suggs said to meet him for breakfast this time, the restaurant across the street, Habeas Cibus. She's seen the place, but she's never been inside. A foreign name like that and crowds of men in striped suits make her antsy. She worries about what to wear, if the place has rules about that. A dress to be safe, she decides. Not a new one, though. Something she can wear to work afterwards and not worry about dye or chemical spots. An hour ago she got a call, an urgent shampoo-and-set job waiting downstairs at Rodell-Ward.

She slips a light blue, flower-print dress over her head and buttons the front in the mirror. She thinks she's pretty enough, although sometimes she thinks maybe she got pretty too young. She wishes she were brighter when it comes to people, understanding what they do and why. She has this sense that everyone else was born knowing some secret thing that they're not allowed to tell her. In her notebook she writes quotes, snatches of things people say that sound intelligent, scribbling them down like clues.

Suggs is sipping coffee in a corner booth, file folders stacked beside him. One folder—it's hers, she sees—lies open on the table, its long pages flipped up, rolled over the top and tucked under. The lawyer's necktie knot is tugged loose. The wide end lolls across the papers like a second tongue. He's writing, making check marks on the page with his fat ink pen. As Cheryl slides into the booth, the pillow seat breathes cold air on her legs. The lawyer quits what he's doing, and he caps his pen with a snap. He laces his fingers together and tucks his elbows tight against the paunch of his gut. Cheryl tries to cross her legs, bangs a knee beneath the table. Suggs steadies his sloshing cup. Leaning forward, he says, Good morning, Miss Riffle. There's a bourbon breeze in the air.

Cheryl tries to read what's under his fist-ball. She asks, Is that my case?

Indeed it is, he says. His kind of word—indeed. His face gives her nothing.

Let me guess, she says. The judge has to delay us again. Am I right?

Suggs flips her file closed, pats the worn cover like somebody's shoulder. He says, The judge wants this one cleared up. He thinks it's dragged on much too long.

Heat rises in Cheryl's neck. After all, they're the ones who kept delaying, kept making excuses, kept putting it off. She won't say it, though, not to Suggs. The court made him her lawyer. It's confusing, though, because he's not hers, not really. Jerry says Suggs probably fishes with the judge, that they're best buddies behind her back. More times than she can count, Jerry's hunches turn out true.

A waitress comes over and refills the lawyer's cup. She's a slip of a girl, tall and young, her forehead freckled and acne-spotted. She's pregnant—six months, maybe seven—the bulge of her belly hugged tight by a denim skirt. She sets the coffeepot down, pulls a pad from her pocket, and stands near Cheryl, a pencil stub pinched between nail-bit fingers. She asks, Can I get you something?

Coffee, Cheryl says, looking at the pot. And a Pepsi and a fried honey bun. The girl repeats it, and when Cheryl says, That's right, she writes it down. There's a jittery tension in this girl. She feels familiar to Cheryl, like someone she used to be. As the waitress starts back to the kitchen, she drops her pad. She has to stoop sideways picking it up, fumbling it twice before getting a grip and standing again. A few seconds later, she's back at the table. Red-faced, she snatches up the coffeepot she forgot. As she leaves, it occurs to Cheryl that this girl might be the kind of person who could be her friend.

Suggs blows across his coffee and slurps a noisy first sip. He says, Don't you go reminding the judge about who stretched things out.

I won't, Cheryl says. Lord knows, I'm in no rush to do prison time.

Suggs says, Let's not get ahead of ourselves, young lady. You got a lawyer here, don't forget.

She can see she's hurt his feelings. Considering he isn't billing her—she couldn't pay, couldn't afford a hired lawyer, but still, considering that he'd never so much as sent her a bill—she tries extra hard to not disrespect him. She knows how it hurts, fixing hair for free at the county home, getting yelled at by people who don't know better. That's part of the deal. But their relatives, the ones who should still have manners? That's ignorant, plain and simple. So what if Jerry is right? Maybe Suggs does bass-fish with the judge. Still, she wouldn't want Suggs thinking she's ignorant that way.

I know I've got me a lawyer, she says. She reaches across and touches his hand. You're a good lawyer, too, she says. She has no way to know that, not really, no lawyer to compare him to. Still, it seems the right kind of thing to say.

He straightens, clears his throat. Listen, Miss Riffle, he says. If we go to trial, they have to prove this case. You understand that? They have to prove your involvement with that shoebox of drugs.

I'm the one lifted it, she says, like me and Jerry—

Suggs slaps the table. Did I ask you who took it? Did I ask you that?

She hates feeling scolded, hates how it puckers her insides, how it brings tears to her eyes for everyone looking to see. She turns toward the wall, hides her eyes with a hand.

Cheryl, he says. Miss Riffle.

She draws in an unsteady breath and turns back toward him again. His face has a pitying look. It's a look she can't stand. She studies her fingers, pinches the knuckle skin, taps each nail, rubs her thumb on the sensitive center of a palm, pressing hard.

Suggs says, We have several ways we can go with your case. You need to tell me what you want, though, so I'll know how to proceed.

Her brain feels strangely cluttered, yet empty, filled with lots of nothing. She says, What I want?

He says, What you want. His eyes look straight into hers, and she imagines he can read everything in there, can see the horrible mess she is.

I want, she says, not knowing what comes next. I want things to go back like before.

Suggs asks, Before what?

She feels the tears again. This time she can't stop them. She searches her purse for a tissue. The lawyer hands her a napkin, which she takes and turns away.

When Cheryl turns back to Suggs, having finally gotten hold of herself, her coffee, Pepsi, and fried honey bun are there on the table. She's got her own napkins now, and she uses one to wipe her face, to catch the last sniffle under her nose. I'm such a mess, she says.

He looks into what's left of his coffee. It's okay.

I'm sorry, she says.

It's okay, he says again. He picks up the folder. Flipping pages, he asks, Have you ever been evaluated?

A laugh escapes her, and she can't understand why. Evaluated? She says. Sure. Yes. All the time. Is that what you're doing now? She asks. Evaluating me? He's smiling at her, but it's not a real smile. It's not in his eyes.

He gathers up folders and stacks them on his lap. Let me talk to Judge Hawkins, he says, run something by him.

You're leaving?

He says that his next appointment is waiting two booths away. Stay here as long as you want, Suggs says. Take your time. Finish your breakfast. Bring me the check when it comes.

The parking lot at Rodell-Ward is full. Cars are parked down the street, both sides, both directions. Black limousines line the circular driveway. Their tiny green bumper flags flutter like spring leaves in a breeze. Several smokers cluster on the porch, a sunny place, talking. Cheryl drives past the stately old house and circles to the alley behind the place.

The backyard is overgrown, the path shaded by enormous live oaks. Beside the basement door, she puts down her shoulder bag, takes out a sweatshirt, and tugs it on. She shoves the right sleeve up to her elbow, reaches up, and searches with a hand deep among the damp trumpet vines. Out front, the smokers' low banter floats through the air like spoken tunes. In the rough stones, Cheryl's fingers find a tiny alcove, and there the key that Mr. Rodell left for her. She unlocks the door, turns the oval brass knob, and silently opens the door. Inside, she switches on the lights.

The girl waits for Cheryl in a pea green room, a room with a double door. It's a cold room with a sour kind of hospital smell, small like a prison cell. The girl lies waiting there, waiting on a bright metal table. She lies covered head to toe on the table, covered by a sheet the same color as the walls. Cheryl lifts the sheet, pulls it back to see the lifeless face, the shoulders, narrow, bare, the neck jogged oddly to one side, an impossible angle for a neck. The girl looks young, eleven or twelve, her skin a nutmeg color. Although her eyes are closed, a mildly surprised look is on her face. Her full lips seem poised to speak. Her untroubled forehead reflects the room's sickly green light. Her black hair has red-dyed streaks in it. Maroon tips, too. Cheryl touches the hair, rolls a few strands between finger and thumb. It's straight and shiny, but matted now. No injuries to work around. That's good. An arcade photo of the girl, alive and mugging for the camera, is tucked beside her head. Cheryl picks it up. She's younger in the photo. Her hair, not as long, is clipped in tiny bow barrettes. When he called,

Rodell told her, Cheryl, you get all that red out you can. Her momma wants it natural black.

Overhead, the upstairs floorboards creak—people standing, people shifting foot to foot, people filing past another someone's coffin, their voices a low murmuring, a rolling kind of sound.

Cheryl looks around, searching for paperwork. She doesn't want to know how the girl died. It doesn't matter anyway, not now. She doesn't want the dreams, either, the ones that come from knowing. She only wants a name, what to call this girl, how to think of her as she does her hair. She wishes now she'd thought to ask Rodell about a name.

She pulls the sheet back and folds it onto itself at the end of the table. The girl is long boned, slender. Her nail polish matches the streaks in her hair. She has a slight swell of breasts, narrow hips, first signs of private hair. Last signs. She's eleven at most. Maybe ten. Her frail chest is sunken and still. Her knees are knobby, boy-like, scabbed. One knee is slightly bent as if, walking, she'd died midstride.

My name is Cheryl, she says out loud. She touches the soles of the girl's feet, the tender white skin of the arches. She runs a finger along her ankle and calf, past a knee, up a slender thigh. She touches the girl's hand, the fingers cold and stiff, and she imagines how it would feel, this child holding her hand like a mother's.

I'm Cheryl, she says again. I'm here to fix your hair. She leans close, her ear near the girl's lips, and she listens for a secret. In the stainless steel table, she sees side by side two reflections, sees parts of two faces, one cheek, one ear each, falling hair black and light brown on bright metal, one eye alive and open, one closed.

The shampoo smells like apricots. In her hands the suds feel thick and warm. She works the lather in. The girl's head moves slightly side to side. Cheryl rinses, and the suds drain away on the tilted table, drain down plastic tubes to plastic jugs below.

When she looks at the tangle of tubes below that table, Cheryl feels a pang low in her abdomen. She thinks of her own tubes, re- members the pair of dark-faced granny women, their treatments, the gnawing ache for days down there. She was just fourteen then, and still the women said she'd come too late. The root cures hadn't worked, they said, dishonesty in their eyes. Infections, they said, the word like spit on their lips, the devil's own worst kind. She'll bear no children now, they told her mother, not in this life. Amen, her mother answered, and she counted out ten-dollar bills into their waiting hands.

Jerry kicks at the cinder block with his muddy boots, trying to loosen the clods stuck deep in the treads. Rust-colored mud shapes —diamonds—fly out and disappear among the trumpet vines. From heel to toe, he scrapes the soles on the block's gritty edge. After wiping his hand on the back pocket of his jeans, he grips the oval brass doorknob. Silently, he opens the door.

Inside he hears a sound, the whine of a hairdryer. It comes from a room off to his right. He's never been in this place before, not in the basement. Upstairs, yes. Never down here, though. It feels like trespassing, like burglary must feel. He moves quietly. The air feels clammy against his skin. Its sour smell makes him want to burp. He cracks open the double door. Cheryl's back is turned to him, three steps away. He'll step in behind her and before she sees him, before she even knows he's there, he'll clamp his hands on her ribs, dig them in sharp and deep, scare the b'jesus out of her. As he inches the door open, she switches off the hairdryer. The sudden silence is a roar in his ears. A hinge squeaks. She hears, gasps, turns. Her hand flies to her mouth too late to catch a small scream.

I knocked, he says, opening the door fully now.

Don't you ever, she says.

He says, You didn't answer.

The hairdryer, she says, like it's her fault.

He sees the black hair now, the face, the shoulders, the sheet. And who is this?

Cheryl's hand is on his chest, pushing. Out! She says. Now!

He's stronger and stubborn when he wants to be, and he wants to be now. Was he hurting anything? No. Besides, he has reason to be here. He grabs her wrist and pushes it aside, pushes her aside, and goes over to the table.

Jerry, get out!

He lifts the sheet, stoops, and looks under it. She's just a kid, he says.

With small fists Cheryl punches his shoulder. So help me, Jerry, she says. You've got no right.

He backs away, hands up, retreats to the door. What killed her? He asks. Cheryl pushes him, and this time he lets her, stumbling back into the hall.

She says, You don't belong here.

He asks, You got any idea what time it is?

You'll get lunch when I get home, she says. Fix a sandwich if you're hungry.

Your lawyer called, he says. That's why I came. That was the reason, he says, if you must know, why I came all the way out here. Jerry turns then and starts to leave.

Wait, she says. She grabs his sleeve. What'd he say?

That jackass judge wants to see you today. One o'clock. He wants me there, too.

Cheryl's face takes on its confused look. Jerry wonders if he's saying too much, talking too fast for her peanut-butter brain. He shows her his wristwatch, pushes it up close to her nose. Almost twelve thirty, babe, he says. She doesn't answer. He says, What it means is we've got thirty minutes to get there. Hurry up and finish Miss Stiff.

She says she'll be five minutes, that she's putting final touches on the girl's hair, the red streaks and maroon tips.

As soon as Jerry walks to the water fountain, Suggs comes over to where Cheryl is sitting. He says, Tell your boyfriend to keep his mouth shut once we get inside. It's a useless thing to tell Jerry, she knows, but she says, Okay. They're in the courthouse hallway, waiting on hard wooden benches. And you, Suggs says, remember you only answer what you're asked. Nothing more.

She nods.

I'll call when we're ready, Suggs says, and he goes into the judge's office. She thinks of the girl on the table, how she's lying there dead in this world, her hair whatever her mother or a stranger, a hairdresser she never knew, decides it should be. Cheryl hasn't stopped thinking of the girl, not once since leaving her there.

Jerry comes back. His footsteps sound hollow in the marble hall. He plops down on the bench, pushes close beside her, and spraddles his legs. His knee nudges hers. He says, Let me show you something. From his pants pocket, he pulls a root. It's shaped like three fingers joined by a large knuckle. Tendrils stick out of the thing everywhere. She covers it with her hands.

That's ginseng, she whispers.

Not just any sang, he says, pulling it free. See that shape? Don't it look like an elephant?

She doesn't think so, but it's not something to argue about. Where'd you dig it?

He whispers, Boone Forest, over by Spivey. Spent the morning scouting around.

It's illegal, she says, digging sang there.

He slides it back into his pocket. Can't no one prove where it came from, he says. Besides, you know what foreigners pay for wild-grown sang that's animal shaped?

Jerry, she says, I want nothing to do with that.

Suit yourself, he says.

Cheryl can tell by his voice he's hurt. He may sulk about it, but she's not going along with this scheme, not while she's looking at jail. Jerry stands and stuffs his hands in his pockets. He hunches his shoulders to his ears, and he wanders down the hall. He's still standing there, studying the photos on the wall, a minute later when Suggs comes out and calls them into the judge's chambers.

Judge Hawkins sits pushed back from his desk. He isn't wearing his robe, just pants and white shirt and starry blue necktie. He looks shorter now, wide, his face loose like bread dough. A lawyer named Embry sits to one side. He's the gourd-shaped one who prosecuted Jerry before. Jerry gives him his dagger look. He doesn't say anything, though, not yet.

Judge Hawkins has more files than Suggs. They're stacked on his desk. He says, Let's get on with it.

Embry says, Your Honor, the Commonwealth has offered to drop several charges against Miss Riffle, in exchange for a guilty plea on count six of the indictment.

Hawkins flips pages, adjusts his glasses. And count six is what? Yes, here, second-degree drug trafficking. These were prescription drugs?

Suggs says, Yes, Your Honor.

Cheryl fights the urge to explain, to tell that she's the one who stole them in the first place, a shoebox full, that she deserves as much jail time as Jerry, maybe more.

The judge says, Mr. Suggs tells me there are circumstances. He's talking to Embry, but he glances at Jerry, too. Jerry's got the root elephant out of his pocket. He holds it low, below the desk so the judge can't see. He rubs it with a thumb like he doesn't even care.

Embry says, Your Honor, we're prepared to recommend probation for Miss Riffle, two years, with a stipulation that it include behavioral evaluation and counseling.

Jerry jumps up. That's bullshit, he says. He waves the root like a floppy finger.

The judge says, Sit down, son. Put a sock in it.

Jerry says, Two years? I only got eight months.

Cheryl's on her feet. She grabs his arm, pulls him back to his chair. Probation, she whispers. The guy said probation.

Jerry's chest shrinks like a balloon taken out in the cold.

Cheryl says, I can keep my jobs? Then, remembering what her lawyer said, she clamps a hand over her mouth. She mouths a *sorry* to Suggs and sits back in her chair.

Suggs says, I'll confer with my client. We'll let you know.

I want this case cleared today, Hawkins says, standing. Five o'clock.

Embry stands, too, and says, Paperwork will be on your desk in an hour, Your Honor, ready for Miss Riffle's signature.

We'll talk in the hall, Suggs whispers to her. Jerry, you too.

What a circus, Jerry says when they're outside. Cheryl knows he's fed up about something. Tell me this, he says to Suggs. Why drag me down here, make me sit next to the bastard who sent me away. I've done my time. I never need to see him again.

Cheryl wishes he hadn't come, for his sake and for hers.

Suggs says, You both need to understand the options. There's a strange look on Suggs's face, one Cheryl can't figure out.

Jerry says, There's no contest. She'll take the parole.

It's probation, Suggs says.

Jerry says, Okay, probation. She can tell he's pissed about her lawyer playing big shot with him.

The thing about probation, Suggs says, looking straight at Jerry, is she can't be having contact with convicted felons.

The hall goes silent.

Jerry says, They can't do this. Can they?

Cheryl says, Me and Jerry, we live together.

You're not married, though, Suggs says. Not now.

That makes a difference? She asks.

To the law, it does, Suggs says.

Cheryl finds a bench and sits. If I take their probation, she says, I've got to move out?

Suggs comes over and sits sideways by her. No contact means no contact, he says. His eyes are steady on hers. She wonders if he's working some kind of telepathy.

I don't know, Cheryl says, her mind a complete swirl.

Suggs says, Think about it. Talk it over, you two. He looks at his watch and says, Their offer's good till five.

The woman who seats them at Habeas Cibus reminds Jerry of the prosecutor, Embry, the way she looks at them. She leaves them with menus and water. All Jerry wants is something to eat, something sweet and syrupy, something solid and wholesome to nourish him. Waffles, maybe, and blueberry syrup. He's had enough of weasel words, enough slanted options, enough of getting shoved from seventeen different directions. He can tell Cheryl is thinking. She hasn't said one word since they crossed the street.

The waitress, a skinny kid with scads of ripe acne on her face, comes over. She's pregnant as hell and her ring finger is naked. The girl ignores him and smiles at Cheryl, who says, Back again, as if the girl's taking attendance with her pencil and pad.

Jerry orders the waffle and coffee, Cheryl a double cheeseburger, Pepsi, and fries. When he gets back from the men's room, their drinks are already there.

It's not fair, Cheryl says, peeling paper off her straw.

Damn straight, he says. He bongos the table, the chrome edge, with his hands. We can't, he says, we just can't let them run our lives.

Damn straight, she says back at him. She pokes her straw into the Pepsi and ice cubes, stirring and tinkling the drink.

It gives Jerry a good feeling inside, hearing her say it. He's always thought of her as someone special, this first wife of his.

Babe, he says carefully, watching her face. Say we did get married again.

No! She says. She's not fooling about it now.

I'm just saying, he says, just saying if we did. What could they do then? Think about it, Cheryl. They'd be screwed. What could they do?

She says like a groan, Jerry, I can't. You know marriage never works for me.

He says, Maybe this time.

She laughs like it's a sad joke, and she says, Every time, I'm miserable.

He says, That was before.

Jerry, I can't, she says. Don't ask anymore.

He takes out the ginseng root, makes it hop across the paper placemat, makes it look at its reflection in the steel napkin dispenser. His mind is working on something. He catches himself humming. You tell me what then, he says.

I don't know, she says. Her eyes start to go wild. We'll go somewhere, she says, but she says it like she doesn't really believe it herself. We'll pack and move, not tell anyone, Somerset maybe, or Louisville.

He laughs at her. You think they won't find you? You look for work, and you're in their computers. They'll find you, and now you're in for serious prison time. An idea is breathing inside him now, alive and wanting out.

Cheryl says, Then *what?* You tell me.

He says, Guess. She can't. He thinks and then says, Here's a hint. It's right in front of you. She isn't even looking now. He says, It's right under your nose.

Cheryl's eyes are empty. She doesn't have a clue in that head of hers, not one idea. Like always, he's the one left to do the real thinking.

The food comes, his waffle, thinner than the menu picture, a ball of butter sliding off. There's a tiny shot glass of blueberry syrup, not nearly enough. Her burger is open, surrounded by curly fries. Before she can slather on ketchup, he grabs one to try.

Okay, Jerry says when the waitress leaves. Here's what we do. We take this crap they're giving us, and we make us some lemonade. Your sister living in Richmond? We say you're living with her.

Cheryl's head tilts birdlike. She's interested. But I'm not?

Jerry says, That's the beauty. We're camped out together in Boone Forest, the two of us, and we're digging a fortune in sang. This piece here, the one I dug this morning? Twenty-five bucks, maybe thirty. This guy I know, he'll buy all we can dig. Just imagine, two of us living out there every day. We're moving around. Can you imagine it? We're moving around, and we're digging a fortune right out of the ground.

Cheryl twirls a curly fry like a corkscrew streamer and flips it into her mouth. He can tell she doesn't get it yet, doesn't see the beauty of his plan. She says, It's illegal, digging sang in a national forest. Right?

He says, Anyone asks, we say we're campers. We'll even get a legal camp permit. We'll hang it up on our tent. Our sang stash, we'll hide it up a tree for when the rangers come poking around.

She says, There's millions of acres out there.

He says, Millions of trees.

In her face, Jerry could see the splendor of his idea, how it fills her with new hope, fills her head to toe with glorious possibilities. That last morning lying on his Blackburn bunk, his intuition had been right.

Cheryl closes her hamburger and flattens it with her palm and takes a bite. And Myrtle, she says through the food, imagine her out there catching a million crickets and cicadas and mice, bringing them all proud to show me.

Jerry says, Any fool knows you can't take a cat to live in the forest. A dog, maybe yes. Cats aren't like that.

She puts the burger down, wipes ketchup from her lips with the back of her hand. She says, Myrtle has to come, too. I'm all she's got. We can put her on a leash or zip her in the tent. Either way, she's got to come.

Jerry takes his fork and knife and rips the waffle into dry, ragged pieces. He says, I don't know about you, Cheryl. He says, Here

I do all this for you, do it all so we can stay together. And you? You complicate things. You make up roadblocks like nothing in this world matters but you. He pushes his plate away, suddenly sick of the food. He drops his fork and knife on top and pours syrup over everything. He tips the shot glass upside down in the mess, and he squishes it to make his point.

Cheryl straightens, sits schoolteacher stiff, and she stares at him, really stares. He knows he's gotten to her, even though she's not crying yet.

Miss Pizza-faced Waitress decides to come by right then and ask so sweetly is their food okay. They're trained to ask, he knows, so they'll get a decent tip. But he can tell for a fact that this has more to do with what's going on, the discussion about the cat. She's got this know-it-all look spread across her festered-zit face. Not for one minute does she fool Jerry. The little sneak is showing them up in this backhanded sort of way.

You want a tip? He asks straight-faced. She looks surprised, doesn't answer. Here's a tip, he says. Buy yourself some maternity clothes, he says. And get yourself a husband, too. Fast.

The girl whirls around and goes. Jerry glances over. Cheryl's face is frozen into a weird kind of mask. She doesn't get the joke, which any fool with a sense of humor would. She isn't even trying. Instead, she tilts the napkin dispenser, and she stares at her reflection until the mask starts to melt. He tries to think how to explain it to her, how it's funny, what he said to the girl about a tip. Cheryl tosses her napkin. It lands on the table like a parachute. Right away she grabs it again. Her brain, he thinks, must be melting, too.

We don't even know her name, Jerry, she says. She slides out of the booth, and before he can say, Hey wait, she chases after the waitress, who's already halfway across the room. It occurs to him then how birdbrained women can be, how amazingly strange, women like his first wife and this waitress.

She catches up with the girl. Even though their backs are turned his way, Jerry would lay odds the waitress is bawling. Sure enough, Cheryl hands the girl her napkin to use on her face. For a minute they stand right there. People coming and going from the kitchen have to walk around them. Cheryl and the girl have their heads together, almost touching as they talk. Cheryl scribbles in her notepad. She rips out the page, folds it several times, and she gives it to the girl, who squeezes it in a fist.

Jerry drinks his coffee, and he looks around the booth for his sang root. He moves dishes, shoves aside the napkin dispenser and ketchup bottle, runs a hand along the seat's gritty vinyl crease, pushing the hand as deep as he dares. He stands and pats his pockets twice around. Nothing. He gets down and looks under the table. The root shaped like an elephant is nowhere. Jerry swears, and he slams a fist on his thigh. People turn to look. Their stares feel like ants all over his skin. He sits again, drinks his coffee, thinking.

When Cheryl finally comes back, Jerry starts to tell her about the sang root, how it's lost. She straightens the mess on the table, stacking things. She's not really looking for it, though. That much he can tell. We should go, she says when she's finished. She bites her bottom lip the way she does when she's getting ready for something. Jerry doesn't move. I looked everywhere, he tells her, and I can't find the damn thing. Cheryl doesn't answer. She seems different now, an odd version of herself, different in a troublesome kind of way. Jerry feels a new tightness in his head. He says, The sang root is nowhere. He moves closer to her. It's gone, he says. Vanished. As he tells her this, she fools with her fingers, examines her hands on the table, the dye-stained knuckle skin, her ragged fingernails, the necked-down places where rings used to be. Not once does she look up at him. He wishes she'd just cry and be done with it, if that's what she's working up to. What she's doing instead feels too much like being alone.

Lake Charles

My kid brother, Randy, invites me down to the bonfire he and this new girl, Kit, have going beside Bluegill Lake. We call it that—Bluegill Lake—even though it's not named anything on the county map. It's more like a pond than a lake, and not a very big one at that. It's just down the hill from my place, past Randy's trailer, hidden by trees. Every spring, the Kentucky Fish and Game truck comes around and restocks it with bluegill, even though it's mostly on my land. We've got neighbors who'd never allow a trespass like that, a state truck coming inside their fence, no matter what for. I say it's okay, though, as long as they just dump fish and leave.

On the wilderness channel, they're tranquilizing wolves, fitting radio collars around their necks while they're paralyzed so they can study the wolves later, where they go and what they do. It's a rerun, a show I've seen before. But even if it were new, I'd still turn it off and go down there with Randy.

"Bring bug spray," he calls to me from the kitchen. "A blanket, too." He's got beers enough for the three of us, the case of bottles propped against his hip.

I grab my stuff and follow him outside. The sun has dropped below the ridge. The clouds are starting to show color streaks, dull peach and plum. As we cross the meadow and start down the hill, mosquitoes find us. By the time we reach the fire, we're trailing a swarm.

The girl, Kit, knows enough to sit close to the fire, that the bugs can't handle smoke. She's eighteen, or so my brother says. Young girls are normal for Randy, who's going on thirty himself. Older girls are wary of him, the way he sometimes gets. It's the same reason the young ones are attracted; they see his possibilities and miss the risks.

The girl's hair is pushed back from her slender face, held there by a green fabric band. Her lips are full, her eyes tentative and quick. A backpack slumps on the ground near her bare feet, and beside it, a pair of mud-colored sneakers with socks stuffed inside. A blond guitar leans against her thigh, and on a stump nearby, empty bottles are lined up, spotted like bowling pins.

"Meet Ben," Randy says, twisting the cap off a beer. Then he adds, "Our movie star." Already he's told the girl his version of that story. "Meet Kit Carson."

"The name's Carver, Freakbird," she says to Randy. She's using his nickname, what they call him at the radio station, and I wonder what he's told her about that, what he's promised her. The girl gives me a quick, fan-fingered wave. Her eyes seem shy.

Randy horses a fat log around next to her—her right side, naturally—and he sits. Usually I don't notice it, the way his jaw is on that side, the way he's careful about which side people see. But he's been drinking today, and everything he does is a tad delayed.

I find a spot for my folded blanket and sit cross-legged, swatting with both hands through what remains of the swarm around my head. I spray my hands with bug killer and start wiping it on my cheeks, neck, and arms. It's cold on my skin, the smell sour like withered grapefruit. The fire is between this girl, Kit, and me, its flames crackling out from the split pine logs.

No one's talking, so I ask Kit, "You know Kumbaya?" I mean it as a joke—about her guitar, the bonfire, the three of us sitting around like little scout campers.

"Sure," she says, completely serious.

She grabs up her guitar and twists tuning pegs, plucking single strings with her thumb until they sound right to her. Her finger-nails are bit short. They make me look away. She's about ready to start when Randy grabs the guitar neck. "My big brother," he says, "he's yanking your chain, about Kumbaya. He can be cruel that way."

As she pulls free, the strings sound a bad chord. "Fuck your big brother then," she says, settling the guitar on her lap again. Then she plays and sings a little.

Her voice is so soft the words sound like a blessing, not a curse. Her fingertips pluck out a slow, five-note tune. Or maybe it's just a music exercise, a warm-up of some sort. She plays it a second time with one note changed, and then a third time, what might be the first tune again. I can't tell. Randy's the one who knows music, not me.

"Rabbit," Randy says softly, and he points toward a briar thicket.

"Where?" Kit whispers, the palm of her hand quieting the strings.

I spot it and point, too. She still doesn't see it.

"Look for the eye," Randy says.

She pulls up grass and throws it at Randy. "Quit fucking with me."

"It's true," I tell her. "Rabbit shapes are hard to see. What you do is train your eye to find theirs."

Randy makes like he's raising a rifle to his shoulder, drawing a bead on the rabbit. He pulls the phantom trigger. "Broke his legs!" he says.

The girl, Kit, looks sorry for the rabbit, which she still doesn't see. "That's fucking cruel," she says, "shooting to cripple."

Randy says he shot it in the head, or at least he would have if he'd brought his rabbit gun down from his trailer. He throws a stick, and the rabbit bolts into the brush.

The girl looks at me, confusion all over her face.

"What a pure headshot does," I explain, "is make the rabbit kick so hard, jerk so hard, the muscles snap the leg bones. It's this reflex from getting headshot."

"Our Grandpa Coy," Randy says, picking up another stick, "he'd always check for broken leg bones when he skinned and gutted so he'd know it was a pure headshot."

She looks away, looks over at me, and as soon as she does, Randy snaps the stick.

Kit grabs her stomach like she might lose it. "That's sick," she says.

"The rabbit's dead," he says, tossing the pieces into the fire. "Doesn't matter to him either way."

The girl picks up Randy's beer and takes a sip. She's quiet for a minute, hugging her knees, the bottle nestled between her feet. When she finally looks up at Randy and me, her voice has gone sandy. "Last year my ma broke her elbow. For weeks she wore this ugly plaster cast, and she never once let me or my sister or anyone write on it."

Randy waves away mosquitoes, not saying anything.

Kit says, "It's like somehow she got old without ever being young."

Randy reaches over and tugs her shirt neck so he can see down the back. "I bet your old lady freaked when she seen your tattoo."

She jerks away. "Quit," she says, and she slaps at his hand.

"Ben, you ought to see this. The girl's got a goddamn mural on her back."

"Shut the fuck up," she says, and she throws more grass at him.

His back gets rigid. His hands roll up into fists. "Randy," I say, and he stops. "It's just grass, Randy," I say, and he settles back.

"It's just grass," the girl echoes. She slaps something on her arm, brushes it away, and picks up her guitar again.

"You need the spray?" I ask her. I cock my arm, ready to toss the can.

"I'm okay," she says. "Bugs don't bother me much."

"Pass it over here to Sweet Meat," Randy says, reaching across. "They can't get enough of me."

I toss him the can. He sends back a beer. He hasn't offered the girl another one, and I'm thinking maybe I should, even though she's Randy's friend. Maybe they've slept together already. I don't know. Probably they have. That's what I think. Randy's not the kind of brother who announces things like that. But it's not hard to imagine, this girl, Kit, in bed or under a tree somewhere, that wild hair spread everywhere, what she must be like. Tender, I'll bet, even if mosquitoes don't think so. It's been years since I was with a girl that young, more than just to talk to.

Randy's got himself sprayed all over. He's still holding the can, though. I see him reach toward the fire. He grabs a stick and holds the burning end up in the air. He shoots a blast of bug spray across it, and it flares like a flamethrower. Randy howls and looks at Kit to see what she thinks of it. She's ducking, protecting her hair, even though the flame comes nowhere near her. This makes Randy laugh. He shakes the can and sprays it again. Kit jumps to her feet, ready to run. This time the fireball blows out the stick's flame like a birthday candle.

"Quit that," she tells him, and she grabs up her guitar.

"Quit that," he mimics.

"Randy!" I say getting up. "She's scared. Now stop it."

He picks another stick from the fire. "She's scared," he says in a weird cartoon voice. "Now stop it!" He holds the fire toward me, one eye blinked, the spray aimed at my face.

"Don't," I say, but he does. I sidestep, spilling beer, the fireball coming close, a burnt citrus smell everywhere. And then I see the fire running back onto the can, surrounding his hand in a flame glove. He looks at it, mouth open, not believing.

"Randy!" I yell, and finally my brother lets go. The can clatters to the ground. I grab his arm and pour what's left of my beer over his hand. He laughs, and I want to slug him. Kit picks up his beer and gives it to me and I pour it on, too. Randy lifts his hand over his head and catches the last drops coming off in his mouth. "Waste of good beer," he says, his voice in manic flight. He sees the hand now, red and blistering. "Shit!" he says. He shakes the hand as though he'd slammed it in the door. "Fuck-fuck shit!"

"Get some butter on that," Kit says. "There any up at the house?"

Randy kicks the sputtering can toward the fire. Then he starts back up the hill, flailing the hand as he goes.

Kit starts after him. "I'm coming, too."

"No!" he yells. "Stay. I'll take care of it." I can see she's confused, but she knows enough to not fight him on this. As he heads up the hill, she comes back, picks up her guitar from the ground. She gets busy drying it with her shirttail. In the firelight, I can see her eyes, wet and glistening.

I want to say something to his girl, Kit, something that will let her know none of this is her fault, and it's not really Randy's either. But I don't know what it would be. "He wasn't always like this," I finally say.

She doesn't answer, just pushes back some hair that's gotten loose from its band. She gives me a shy, shrugged smile that I can't decode.

"You know him long?" I ask. I wish she'd come closer to the fire.

She shakes her head. "Since yesterday."

"Randy's a piece of work, that's for certain," I say. Right away, I wish I hadn't, him being my brother and all. I think maybe if I tell her about him, she'll understand. Like always, my problem is sorting what to tell from what to hold back.

She glances up toward the house again. The sky isn't dark yet, but it's not bright anymore either. "Maybe we should check on him, Ben." She's got a grip on the guitar neck again, leaning with it against the scaly trunk of a sycamore tree.

I tell her he'll be okay. She shifts from one foot to the other and says maybe she should be going then.

"Stay," I say. "Please stay."

She fools with the ends of her leather-braided bracelet and seems to think about it. "Randy said he had a studio, that I could tape some songs."

"The radio station," I say. "It's where he works. WJCT." He's got a key to the place. Mostly he's the janitor, the handyman. But I don't tell her that part.

"You work there, too?"

"No," I say. "No, I do welding." It's hard work. Technical, too. From the look on her face, you'd think I said ditch digging.

She sputters out a little laugh. "Randy's been playing me for a fool. He told me you was in the movies."

"For a fact," I say. "*Coal Miner's Daughter*. He didn't tell you that part?"

Her eyes come alive. "The Loretta Lynn movie?"

"I was her bratty kid brother."

Her head turns sideways. "Don't shit me."

With my finger I cross my heart and raise a hand to Bible-swear. "Word," I say. "I was nine. You can buy the video at Spivey Variety. They've got copies personally signed by me."

"That is so awesome!" She comes over to where I'm standing, and she reaches out and touches my arm, which makes every hair stand up. "Loretta Lynn," she says. "She nice like they say?"

I remind myself to breathe. I want to tell this young girl, Kit, that Loretta's just that way, that she treated me great, bought me Cokes and sat with me between takes when we filmed. But I don't, because it's nowhere near the truth. "She wasn't there," I say. "This actress, Sissy Spacek, played her in the movie." I don't tell Kit that Sissy Spacek always called me Willie, which was another boy's name, another of Loretta's brothers.

"I knew that," Kit says, "about Sissy Spacek. She was Carrie, too. Tell me, did she sing in the movie?"

"Wasn't any singing while I was there," I say. "Just family stuff, romping and courting with Moony."

Kit pulls a foot up and rests the arch on the notch of the other knee. Now her legs make the number four, which is lucky for me. I want to tell her that, and I would if it didn't sound dumb. "Used to be," she says, "singers didn't write their own songs."

"You write songs?"

She nods. "Some I borrow off the radio." She says it like it's cheating. "Some lyrics I write, but I take the chord patterns from writers like Lucinda. You know who she is, Lucinda Williams?"

I say I do.

"That woman is so absolutely fucking brilliant!" she says. "She lives in Lake Charles. That's in Louisiana." Her gaze goes far away, and she asks me, "You think she records there, too?"

I say I wouldn't know about that.

A few stars are showing in the eastern sky. The mosquitoes are getting bad again, so I tell Kit we should move back by the fire. I follow the girl, watching. Her walk is an inviting kind of dance. She sits on her blanket and leans back on an elbow. I settle beside her on Randy's log and poke the dwindling fire with a forked stick. Sparks shoot straight up toward the early stars. Her dark eyes reflect the fire. I remember the rabbit then, how its eyes looked. It's something I'd rather forget.

"You from around here?" I'm just making conversation.

"Hardly," she says, but she doesn't say where. She rolls onto her hip, and her hand goes to her jaw. "What happened to your brother's face?"

Staring at my hands, I start to tell this girl, Kit, about Randy, how he got like he is. It's always on my mind anyway, every morning while I shave, every morning in the mirror when I stare at another day and think about what I might do.

"Our Aunt Lucy owned this old Plymouth Fury," I say, "and our mother borrowed it one morning. This was over twenty years ago. She called in sick at work to drive Randy, who was seven, over to Somerset to audition for a part in *Coal Miner's Daughter*. She'd seen a flyer taped to the window of Spivey Variety. It said they were looking for local children—six boys and two girls—who looked and sounded Appalachian.

"Randy was the one with talent. Everyone knew that, so our mother borrowed the car to drive him to audition. She wrote me out a school excuse note and packed me along, too." Without even looking at Kit, I can feel her eyes watching me, can feel a brightness inside.

My brother was handsome back then, almost pretty. His cheeks would dimple when he smiled, which he always did. His hair was white-blond like sun-bleached hay. Randy knew all the John Denver songs. He'd sing them from a porch or stage in a loud, steady voice. Or he'd strum a plastic guitar and wiggle like Elvis. That always got a good laugh. And when banjo and fiddle music played, Randy would clog the way Grandpa Coy showed us, his joints all leather-hinged, his back straight like a stick puppet toy.

To this day I remember the drive to Somerset, me in the backseat, my brother in front, sunlight like butter on the beige seatback between us. Randy, who had started second grade, was just beginning to read. So I'd read the role's five lines over and over to him, and he'd repeat them back. He practiced the words all different ways, duck-voiced, loud bullfrog belches, everything. We must have rankled our mother's nerves. At one point she swerved the car off the road, braking hard. She parked the Fury with two wheels on asphalt and two on gravel. She snatched up her shoulder bag, got out, and crossed the ditch to where the weeds were tall. Beside a scrub cedar tree, she sat cross-legged and fumbled open her pack of dark cigarettes. She lit one and held it in front of her, seeming to study the smoke for a sign. Her mouth moved as if she were telling it something or maybe asking. Then she reached into the bag again, took out a can of beer, and popped the lid. Foam streamed out like champagne. Most she caught in her mouth.

"Get your brother out of that hot car," she called over to me, "so he won't get all sweated up."

I did what she said. In the dusty shade beside the car, Randy and I pitched rocks at each other's shoes while we waited for her to finish. "Ma, let's go!" Randy called to her finally.

"One minute!" she yelled back. She raised the can like she was making a toast. "You know drinking and driving don't mix." It's the kind of thing our mother thought was funny.

While we waited, Randy kicked gravel with his heel, scattering stones and raising a small cloud of dust. "She's making me late," he said, loud enough for her to hear.

"One minute, sweetie." She stood, drained the can, and then stabbed what was left of her cigarette through the lid hole. Coming back to the car, she dropped the can in the ditch. "Let's go, let's go, let's go," she said, as though we were the ones delaying things.

Why I remember that ride to Somerset so clearly, I can't say. The audition itself is a muddle in my mind, as is the ride home to Spivey that evening. Memory is funny that way. What I do remember is that, as I waited out in the hall, a man in a tangerine cowboy shirt came over and asked if I'd try saying the lines, too, which I did. He asked three of us to come back and do it again the following Tuesday. All this I tell Kit.

"So you ended up acting in the movie," she says.

"Not right away," I say. "It wasn't until four months later that they came back with all their lights and cameras loaded with film.

If you rent *Coal Miner's Daughter*, you'll see the nine-year-old me running around in high-water pants, acting up a storm."

She's quiet, so I look over at her.

"And?" she says.

"And that's about all." My head is swimming some, but my mouth has gone dry. I get up, fetch two bottles from the case, and I offer her one.

She reaches for the beer awkwardly, stubbing her fingers on the bottle, nearly fumbling it before getting a grip. She twists off the cap with her shirttail. "What I asked," she says, pausing to drink. "What I asked about was Randy's face, his fucked-up jaw."

"Randy's fucked-up jaw," I say back, searching for where I left off. "Right. That's what you asked."

"That's what I asked." She doesn't seem sweet anymore.

"Okay. You rent that movie," I tell her, "and you look closely, and you'll see I hold my right arm in a peculiar way."

"And?"

"I'm telling it my way," I say. "See, this was important, this day I told you about, Randy, Mom, and me riding to Somerset. It's the last time we were all ourselves."

I tell Kit about the day that changed everything. It was a Saturday, early October. Mom was driving me to rehearsal, taking Randy along in case they changed their minds about him. I was behaving, reading in the backseat. From his fort up front, Randy kept raining M&M bombs on me. Finally, I retaliated, kicking the seatback, a nuclear blast that sent him sprawling under the dashboard. As he crawled back onto the seat, our world tumbled wildly. I swear Randy laughed like he was spinning on a carnival ride. Glass exploded and metal crushed in on me. Then a sizzle of steam was the only sound, and the stink of leaking gasoline was everywhere. Later Aunt Lucy told me that we lay there for nearly five hours before a stray glint of sunlight reflecting from mangled chrome caught the attention of a passing state trooper. I don't remember any of that, not as solid memory.

Kit has her knees pulled close to her chest. She reaches over, puts her hand on mine, and pats it like a dog's head. Her eyes look soft again.

"She lived for two days," I say. "I didn't get to see her in the hospital. Lucy said it was best that I didn't, that she wouldn't want it. My collarbone was broken, my knee busted up, and my skin pricked full of glass slivers. Randy wasn't so lucky. His skull fractured. The doctor couldn't stop the brain swelling. The day they buried our mother, Randy went into a coma. He stayed there for another two weeks."

"And his jaw?" she asks, her voice almost a whisper.

"Shattered," I say. "They grafted bone from his hip to rebuild it. Now that he's older and his face grew, his mouth doesn't line up right. He says he'll get it fixed again, as soon as he gets the money."

"I don't think it's that bad," she says, which I know is a lie or she wouldn't have kept asking about it before.

"They can fix his jaw," I say, "but his brain . . . " I stand up, walk to the edge of the pond, and throw my bottle. I loft it high toward the middle and listen for the splash in the dark. "Randy's never been the same," I say when I get back.

"The brain's a funny thing," Kit says. She stares at the shrinking flames, blue ones dancing around yellow in the coals. "I can't fucking do acid. I totally freak."

"He doesn't do drugs." My voice sounds too harsh, not like I mean.

"I'm just saying . . . " She rolls onto her stomach and gets quiet again.

"I read about this man in France," I tell her. "He had this accident, and an iron bar got rammed through his brain, clear through. And he's okay, normal except for this heavy bar stuck through him, which they don't dare take out."

The way Kit looks at me, I know she thinks I made it up.

"But you damage small parts of your brain," I say, "and you're a fence post. Or you've got a hair-trigger. Or you're blind, or maybe worse. Not that my brother's that bad. They gave him electroshocks."

Her face fists up like she's looking at a wound.

"Little shocks," I say, "not like the movies. Still, sometimes he turns into this weird stranger who does incredibly stupid things."

"Freakbird." Kit says, smiling, but not like it's funny.

"That's him."

Her eyes gaze straight at mine. "Why not just fucking leave, Ben? Start fresh somewhere new."

It's the question I ask myself every morning.

"It's not so hard," she says, "unless you make it hard. When I decide it's time to go, I go. Ain't nothing stopping me."

I look at this girl, Kit, and I imagine what it would be like, free and traveling around with someone like her, all the possibilities.

She must read my mind, because she says, "Come morning, I'm hitching to Nashville, then maybe to Lake Charles from there, Lucinda's place." She's quiet again, the only sound frogs talking down by the water. Then she says, "Or maybe you could drive me." It's not even a question, the way she says it.

I remember reading this travel brochure about Nashville, how Loretta Lynn has a ranch nearby, and it's open for tours. They've got this fake coal mine for visitors to go through. Wouldn't that be something, me walking in the front gate of Loretta's ranch, telling everyone who I am, all grown-up now? This is what I'm thinking as I slide down next to Kit on the ground. She pushes her guitar aside and lies back, and I'm beside her. There's a smile in her eyes, and her hand finds my chest, moves on it, sliding down. And right then, I remember my brother and the burn on his hand. The sky is dark except for stars, and I try to think how long it's been since Randy went up to the house, wonder why he hasn't come back down to the fire.

"Ben," Kit whispers, and I look down at her, let myself fall into her. Her lips are softer than I'd imagined, beery and eager for me. Her hair feels wild in my hand, the fabric band coming off, her lips alive on mine. I float in her soft, herbal smell. When the kiss finally ends, Kit gives a small hum like electricity. I remember him then.

"I should check," I say, stumbling to my feet, "on my brother."

She props herself up on an elbow. "What are you worried about?"

It's a question I can't answer.

I leave Kit and the bonfire and start toward the trees and the path up to the house. Just ahead a rabbit darts out, startling me, paralyzing me, snatching my breath away. It zigzags across the trail and vanishes in the dark underbrush. In my legs I feel an ache—sudden, sharp, and bone deep.

The
Accomplished
Son

One summer afternoon when Toby Polk was eleven years old, he found a rag-wrapped pistol hidden in a slot up under his father's workshop bench. At first he thought some stranger must have put it there, a burglar, maybe, or a vagrant passing through. His father, after all, was a quiet man who spent his days alone in the workshop building chairs. To the boy, Earl Polk seemed no more likely to own a pistol than a howitzer. Still, the gun was undeniable, solid in his hands. He considered every possibility, and when he finally decided that it must be his father's, a frizz of energy ran through him. Toby imagined their lives changing again, things somehow returning to the way they'd been before — before Arnel Embry, before his father's wounding, before the hard times came.

He put the handgun back, then slid it out again. How perfectly it fit, as if the slot were built just for this gun. Six months before, his father, still clumsy in his wheelchair, had hired a carpenter. Together they remodeled the workshop behind the family's Lily Road home. They widened doorways and lopped lengths off the angle iron legs of the radial arm saw and wood lathe. They built ramps in the shop, in the house, and in between. It was then, the boy decided, that his father must have chiseled the pistol slot.

Toby turned the thing over in his hands. The bright and oily heft of the pistol surprised him. In years to come, he would know it as a .38 Special, nickel plated, a dreamer's weapon, perfect for his father. But on that hot Sunday afternoon, as the boy crouched in crisp shavings of pine and cherry wood, he knew only that this was a powerful thing and that the sensation he felt holding it was a pleasurable one. He wrapped the pistol again and put it back where he'd found it.

Toby didn't tell his mother, and he didn't tell Mike, the younger brother from whom he'd been hiding that afternoon. He kept the knowledge to himself, a private nugget, a secret charm of sorts.

In the next few weeks Toby would sometimes dream that his father, .38 in hand, rose up from his wheelchair. Balanced precariously, strangely invisible on his flimsy legs, he'd kill Arnel Embry, the man who had launched a thin metal dart from a pistol crossbow and paralyzed him, had sentenced him to life in that chair. Some nights Toby dreamed that his father tucked the muzzle under his own chin, and, draping a plastic shower curtain over his head to contain the mess, pulled the trigger. And some nights he dreamed that his father, joystick wheelchair revved up and power geared, pursued Toby's mother through the house and into the yard, bullets flying wildly, his aim spoiled by bumpy ramp joints.

Army Specialist Tobias Polk, just back from Iraq, remembers all this as he drives across Kentucky. It happened twelve years ago. The sun, low ahead and rising, burns red through June fog. Beside him, his wife, Inez, is buckled in. She adjusts the visor and loosens the Camry's shoulder belt around the ripe bulge of her belly. She says it's safer this way, safer for the baby she carries inside, leaving the belt slack across her.

Polk's six-month tour in Iraq, his third, has been shortened by a month. He'll be here in the world for the birth. His unit is in Kuwait now, decompressing, recharging before going back — Fallujah this time, if rumors prove true. He doesn't talk about any of this, not with Inez.

Polk's tooth, a molar, starts aching again. He takes out a small vial of clove oil, gets a drop on his finger, and rubs the gum. They'll be back in Arizona next week. He'll see a dentist then, have the damn thing pulled, once this family business is wrapped up.

As he drives, Polk stays alert — alert to other cars, to a small white pickup truck and a cadre of motorcycles, to a black plastic trash bag beside the roadway. He accelerates past a derelict Olds Cutlass abandoned in the breakdown lane. Freshly patched pavement disappears beneath the Camry's wheels. He squeezes the steering wheel. Polk has survived by being aware of such things. All his wife knows to worry about is seat-belt safety for their child.

"Do you miss it?" she asks. "Kentucky?"

Polk glances over. She has a cherub's profile, all upturn and roundness. An Arizona girl, her skin keeps its tan even in winter. Her hair is spiky and short, bleached platinum this week. He enjoys looking at her, feels calmer when he does. He reaches across and touches her belly. He wants to love this child she carries. On the first ultrasound, Inez thought she saw the nub of a penis. Later ones haven't shown it, though. He mulls this endlessly on nights when he can't sleep, trying to imagine it — Toby Polk, father of a daughter. It seems unreal.

"Do you?" Inez asks again. "Miss it?"

"Kentucky? Sometimes." He draws his hand back. "When my parents divorced, that part sucked."

"You don't talk about it."

"Shit happens," he says. He rummages in the console, clatters plastic cases, searching for music to play.

"You were happier," Inez asks, "once she left, once she took you to Phoenix?"

"What do you think? New state, new school, her scrambling for work, me all of fifteen? That sound like a picnic to you?" He remembers school fights, battles at home. "Can we talk about something else?"

"I'm just asking, Toby." She wears her hurt expression now. "Married people do that, have conversations, talk about things."

"And I've told you before." Polk lets the console lid slam shut. "Life was shit for Mike and me. And when we moved in with Ma's jerk boyfriend . . . ," he says. "What the fuck. You met Barry. You know."

Not half of it, really, does she know.

Or need to know.

The roadway dips. Fog drifts across in wispy patches. On an overpass ahead, two boys straddle bicycles. Their hands are stuffed in the pockets of camouflage jackets. Polk's mouth goes dry, the pain inside a dull ache. His hands tighten on the steering wheel. He waits, waits, waits, and then he swerves the car into the breakdown lane.

Inez lurches sideways, grabs the door handle as they speed beneath the boys. "Jesus, Toby! What was that?"

"Couple of punks," he says, "loitering on the overpass."

She's quiet for a minute. Then Inez reaches a hand across the console, and she squeezes his shoulder. It's a gesture of love, he thinks, or maybe sympathy. He can't tell for sure anymore.

"Sorry, babe," he says.

Her hand slides to the back of his neck. Her fingers work on the tension there. "It's okay, Toby," she says. "Honest. It's okay."

———————————

Toby steers the car up the gravel driveway and parks behind his brother's rust-rotted pickup truck. Mike Polk pushes a sputtering lawn mower across the splotchy yard of the house on Lily Road. An oily exhaust hangs overhead in a flat blue cloud.

"This is it?" Inez asks, lowering the car window and shading her eyes.

"This is it," Toby says. He shifts into park and sets the brake.

"I imagined it bigger."

"It was," he says, "when I lived here." He gets out and goes around the car to help his wife. She's already out, stretching, hands braced low on her back when he gets there.

Mike stops the mower long enough to wipe his brow with a sleeve. He shouts over, asks if they've gone by the cemetery.

"Not yet. This here's Inez," Toby shouts back.

Mike waves and tells them he'll be done mowing in two shakes, that he wants the place looking good for them. "Go right in. Make yourselves homely," Mike tells them, and a stupid grin cracks his face. "Help yourselves to whatever you need."

Toby reaches into the car and lifts out his wife's shoulder bag. Mike yanks the starter cord and the mower clatter-roars again. The sudden racket startles Toby, sends an electric buzz down his back and legs. Across the yard, the machine kicks up dust whorls.

Inez grabs his arm. "Some welcome," she says in his ear.

He takes her hand, squeezes it lightly. "Don't," he says. "Okay?"

Her gaze goes to the gravel between their feet. She draws a breath like a diver getting ready, then lets it out in a slow, hissing leak. It's her way of relenting.

Toby shoulders the bag strap, and he leads Inez past his brother's truck, up three leaf-stained concrete steps to the side door. He pauses there, the doorknob familiar in his hand, and he looks back. The long ramp is gone. What remains of it is piled out back, the weathered lumber a haphazard stack. Bent nails point every which way.

"Arnel Embry came to the funeral," Mike says in the kitchen. He opens the refrigerator, stoops to look in. His long hair, still wet and comb-streaked after his shower, slips like a curtain across his cheek. "You drink beer?" he calls to Inez. They left her in the front room with a photo album.

"Gave it up." Her voice has a drifty sound, as if she's distracted. "Pregnant, you know."

Mike grabs two bottles from the refrigerator, hands one to Toby. "I shoved the old man's stuff to the back," he says. "Maybe I should throw it out." He looks at Toby as if it's a question.

"Embry showed up?" Toby says, twisting the cap off. "Some nerve."

"Nine people came to his goddamn funeral." Mike holds up fingers. "Nine, and that includes me, and it includes the preacher, and it includes the fucking mortician."

"But Arnel Embry?" Toby says.

Mike huffs out a sickly laugh. "At least he came."

Toby takes a drink and looks around the kitchen. "He died here?"

Mike points his bottle at the chrome-rimmed table. "Over there." He starts toward the front room. In the doorway he says, "Embry asked about you, why you weren't there."

"What balls," Toby says.

In the front room, Mike drops into their father's chair. "I told him you were busy snipering some Taliban."

Toby Polk winces. "Wrong country," he tells Mike. "Different bad guys." The air in the room is viscous now, hard to breathe. He goes to a window, opens it, and leans on the sill looking out. His pulse throbs in his tooth, his jaw, everywhere in his head.

Inez has his wrist, then his hand, and she tugs him back to the couch to sit beside her. She takes up the photo album again and opens it across their legs. "You were one darling boy," she says. He feels the sting of her pity. It's the last thing he wants from a wife.

———

Long past midnight, Toby Polk lies on a cot in his childhood bedroom. Inez sleeps in a twin bed nearby. Nighttime sounds filter through the window screen, a dog barking at the night, crickets chirping back and forth, a rooster mistaking moonlight for an early dawn. In the ceiling cracks and textures, Polk finds familiar faces, ones he'd found there as a boy — gnarled witches, midgets, and gnomes.

Despite the beers, he hasn't slept, can't sleep, like so many other nights. In Iraq they've got combat pills to keep you awake three days straight — longer if you need. And they've got pills for sleeping afterward. Trouble is, lately those don't work. And now the damn tooth makes sleep impossible.

In his mind, Polk replays that evening's visit to his father's grave, the sad look of the place, how a kind of rage rose up in him just seeing it, a nothing place, hardly there at all. It shouldn't bother him so. He knows that. He worries that his life is coming loose again, imagines himself careening, crashing. Each time his mind drifts toward sleep, a jolt of dread yanks him back, even more alert. Panic lurks behind his eyes, waiting for any brief unguarding. It could happen soon, he knows, very soon, any moment now.

The throb is deep in his jaw now, its taste like tin under his tongue. He remembers the time he fractured a front tooth in a fight with Lonnie McCray. He must have been seven then. Maybe eight. His mother wrapped two cloves in a fresh mullein leaf. She told him to hold it against the tooth, said the pain would go away. Instead it got worse. So his father took him back to the workshop, and he brought out a cloth pouch. Inside he kept dried jimsonweed.

"Our secret," Earl Polk said, and he waited for his boy to nod that it was. Then he packed a pipe and lit it for Toby to puff. The smoke tasted harsh. At first Toby coughed. The world got weird then, and he thought he was floating, his pain drifting miles away. He slept, and next morning his mother shook him awake and drove him to the dentist in town.

A dog barks outside. Inez rolls onto her side and mumbles into her pillow. Polk swings his legs off the cot, and he sits in the dark room. For a minute he watches the slow in and out of his wife's steady breathing. Then he gets up. He quietly gropes for his pants, shirt, and shoes. Carrying them, he feels his way down the dark hallway to the kitchen.

He rinses his mouth with Jack Daniels, a bottle he's found deep in the refrigerator. He spits the mess into the sink. It's no help for the pain. So he pours more, three fingers, and gulps it from the glass. It burns his throat going down. Then he pours more and sips as he dresses.

The key is still hidden low along the door frame. Polk takes it from its nail. In the dark, he jiggles the key into the padlock and twists. The lock pops open, the sound solid as a stone in his hand.

He unhooks the padlock, slips the hasp off the staple, and opens the workshop door.

Inside, he flips the wall switch. It takes a moment before the fluorescent lights blink on. In that last dark moment, he remembers how it was, the benches tall, shelves high, the lathe still long-legged, back before things went bad, before the ramps. Then the lights buzz, flicker, come on fully bright. Chairs without seats huddle together like leggy children. Chisels are scattered across the bench. A chair back is clamped in the bench vice. Rubber straps bind the uprights to carved rungs, the glue set long ago.

He steps around a pile of swept shavings and sawdust. He opens drawers, searches shelves, and he finds the old pipe in a low nail bin. There's no cloth pouch anywhere, though. Polk draws in the empty pipe, then flings it away and turns to leave.

At the door he stops. He goes back to the workbench and kneels there. One hand grasps the edge for balance. He ducks down and reaches up. His free hand finds the slot and the rag-wrapped pistol. Old sawdust drifts down as he slides the thing out. A stale smell is in his nose, a dry taste in his mouth.

He folds back the rag. Under fluorescent lights, the .38 Special shines silver bright. The cylinder, heavy with cartridges, spins easily under his thumb. It feels reassuring in his hand, a calming thing. Polk's breathing settles now.

———

The June night sky is clear, the stars bright away from streetlights. Polk wears the denim jacket he found hanging in the shop, its cuffs hiked up on his wrists, sleeves worn ratty by wheelchair rails. The pistol is tucked behind him, beneath his belt, snug against his spine. With each step, he feels a solid kneading.

Polk reaches Arnel Embry's place with no memory of walking there, no sense of intent. Still, it feels inevitable. The pain in his mouth has become a wet throbbing again. The tooth must be abscessed now, poison leaking into his blood.

The house is split-level, white clapboard, a wide garage extending to one side. The lawn and blacktop driveway slope up to the house. A privet hedge tall as a man runs along the roadway and up either side of the yard. The house is dark except for an upstairs window where a pink night-light glows.

Polk walks past, crosses the road, and settles onto the dark slope of a weedy hill. Dew soaks his blue jeans. A shiver races up his back and across his chest. He remembers the heat of Baghdad, how he'd crave a chill like this as he lay waiting, helmeted, body armor zipped and snapped. He'd baste there in his own sweat drippings, eyes stinging, his M-24 sniper rifle braced and waiting for another kill. Polk is an expert marksman, one of the best. And waiting is something he's always done well.

Lights inside the house come on at five fifteen, first one room, then another. A dingy Plymouth chugs by, slowing slightly. The driver lobs a rolled newspaper toward the driveway. Polk raises an arm, starts to turn away, to duck, imagining the thing exploding. Instead, it lands with a dull thud on the asphalt, just a newspaper after all. A queasy feeling washes over him, so damned jumpy, so chicken-shit back here in the world, all these miles from war. Relax, he tells himself. Block everything else and stay focused. You can do this.

The sun is up, hanging somewhere below the trees, when Arnel Embry comes hurrying down the driveway. A tall, ruddy-faced man, Embry is narrow across the chest and shoulders, thick around the waist. He's dressed for work, a lawyer — tan slacks, blue shirt, striped necktie, red and blue.

Polk crosses the road quickly and skirts the hedge. He's only a few feet away when the man, stooped to pick up his newspaper, sees him. Embry straightens slowly, momentary confusion showing on his face. "Morning," Embry says, and he turns and starts back up the drive.

"Arnel Embry," Polk says, stopping him.

Embry turns, peering at him, the rolled newspaper held like a club. Then his face brightens. "Toby Polk," he says, stabbing two fingers at him. "Am I right? Your brother said you were coming to town. Listen, I'm really sorry about your father. Earl was a good man. Like I told Mike, it's senseless, him dying young."

"Senseless," Polk says.

"You missed the funeral."

"I was overseas," Polk says. "The army didn't get word to me in time." He hates that he's explaining.

Embry gives out a grunt. "That's rough."

"How come you showed up?"

The expression on the lawyer's face tightens, and his gaze steadies on Polk. "It's a funeral, son," he says. "You let bygones be."

"You know damned well that's not what he'd have wanted."

"What do you want from me, Toby? Why are you here?"

"Yesterday, I went to the cemetery," Polk says, beside him in the driveway now. "Everybody near him, every grave in the section, they've got upright tombstones. My old man, he'd bought himself a lay-down-flat one, the kind they just mow over. They don't even have to trim. Grass clippings already cover the thing."

"You want a different gravestone —"

"No. What I'm saying is that's how he was. He couldn't let things go, but he didn't do anything about them either." Polk moves closer now, inches from the man's face. "I'm someone else. You walk into my father's funeral like it doesn't matter, like you never did a thing, like it wasn't you started all the damage."

"It was an accident," Embry says, "a fucking accident."

"You show me," Polk says. His body feels its adrenaline now. The pain in his mouth hardly matters. "Show me exactly how it happened. Make me understand."

Embry steps back and glances at the house, the front door. For a moment Polk thinks he might bolt. But then Embry's hands come together. His thumb works deep in the palm of the other, rubbing the soft middle. "It was this pistol crossbow," he says, "a Belgian design, eighteenth-century replica."

"Show me." Polk grabs the man's elbow, gives him a shove up the driveway.

Embry stumbles. "I busted it up, Toby," he says, regaining his balance. His hands lay open to the sky now. "I didn't want the damn thing around."

"So get another. Show me with that," Polk says. "All those trophies you've won, all those ribbons shooting crossbow, don't tell me you don't have others."

In the garage, hunting bows with sculpted shapes, strings slack, hang from pegs along a side wall. Beneath them, the fletched ends of arrows protrude from green plastic tubes. Several crossbows are mounted along the back wall, shoulder-fired models with wood and plastic stocks, and off to the side, three smaller ones with pistol grips. Embry touches a metal-handled model. "Something like this, except the Belgian had a carved oak stock. More like a dueling pistol."

Polk lifts the weapon from its wall hooks, slides his hand along the body, studies the aluminum dart rail, the woven wire string, the black-anodized cocking lever. "This the safety?" he asks, diddling a switch he knows must be.

"The Belgian didn't have one," Embry says. "A safety."

Polk picks up a metal dart. It's long like a pencil but slender, plastic-fletched in canary yellow. The tip end is surprisingly heavy. He probes the point with a fingertip.

"Careful," Embry says. "They're sharp."

Polk holds the tip to the light, squinting. Then he trails it across the back of his hand. Behind the point, the scratch brightens and a string of small blood drops appears. It's bright red, not nearly black as he'd expected.

"Like I said . . ."

Polk mounts the dart on the rail and hands the uncocked weapon to Embry. "Show me, Arnel." His voice starts to tremble. "You show me how this thing happened."

For a moment Embry looks at the pistol crossbow as if it's something he's never seen. Then his gaze comes up, and his head tilts slightly. Polk returns the look, waiting. Something like a smile assembles itself on the lawyer's face. "You have a right to know," he says. He grabs a candle stub from the bench and walks to the door. "Come out back."

The yard is wide, the air outside noisy with morning birds. Saplings in mulched circles are staked and wired upright. The lawn fades into dark woods at the back, where a dozen straw bales are stacked. A paper target shaped like a man is draped across the center bales. It is peppered with holes.

Embry sights the weapon. "You been back long?" he asks.

It takes Polk a moment to understand he means Iraq. "Few days," he says.

"Takes time," Embry says. He rubs the candle along the crossbow's dart rail. "I was in Vietnam—Da Nang. Twenty-seventh Marines."

Toby Polk tries to imagine this man young and lean, tries to imagine him without the gut, imagine him in uniform, in camouflage and heat. "Different war," he says.

"You guys are heroes," Embry says. "That's what I say."

When Polk doesn't answer, Embry adds, "It's not everyone can fight a war." He sights down the dart. "Not everyone's got the constitution."

"That's it," Polk says. "The constitution." He turns Embry's word over in his mind, trying to make it fit. It doesn't, not exactly. Polk knows inside who he is, what he is, knows it better than words can say.

The lawyer slides the dart along the track. "You kill anyone?"

Polk shrugs in a practiced way. "Who knows?" he says. He does know, though. He remembers every one, remembers them clearly. Each time his eyes close, he sees them, the crouched silhouettes of rooftop fighters. They drift into his realm, his night-vision world, a place all scintillating and green. They come believing in the hiding power of Iraqi nights and dance briefly with his silent crosshairs. Then the slow trigger-squeeze, and they fling dark emerald splatters across bright cinder-block walls. This knowledge Polk won't give up, not to Embry. He hasn't even told Inez, not yet. Maybe he never will.

"Vietnam was jungles," Embry says. He straightens and draws air into his chest. "Over there we shot all the time, single rounds, bursts, not really aiming. It was jungles everywhere, and Charlie was clever. He never left bodies behind. So we never knew."

Polk's voice is a taut whisper. "Maybe my father was your first kill?"

"Jesus, Polk! It was an accident! Your father said so. Sheriff Tate, too." His grip tightens on the weapon's handle, tendons moving beneath skin. "Besides, he didn't die."

"Not fast, maybe. Not that day or year."

"I'm sorry. You've got to know," Embry says, his expression crumbling now. "It was just this horrible, freaky thing."

"He died slow," Polk says, the words tight in his throat. "He took twelve years doing it—"

"You can't blame —"

"— twelve years turning rancid in that wheelchair, watching his wife walk away with his sons, watching her leave for some sack-of-shit boyfriend still tooled to satisfy. That, and he'd beat on us when she thought we needed it."

Embry straightens again, making himself tall. "You'd better leave."

"My father's dead now. His grave is marked by a fucking apology of a tombstone. Who gives a shit anymore? And here you come, parading yourself at his funeral like a friend, as if none of us matter, as if his life didn't really end years ago."

"You're trespassing, son," Embry says. He turns and faces Polk, the metal dart in the track pointed his way. "Leave now."

"This how it happened?" Polk asks.

"I'm done talking." Embry's hand steadies.

"You forgot to cock it."

Embry works the crossbow's cocking lever and threads the wire string in the slot. "That seem right to you?" the lawyer asks, showing it. "Now go!"

Polk reaches over and releases the safety catch. "There," he says. He steps back and opens his jacket.

The crossbow wavers in Embry's hand, the aim loose. "Louise!" he calls hoarsely. "Louise! Call Sheriff Tate."

Polk turns and reaches a hand back under the denim jacket and brings out the .38. "This thing doesn't have a safety," he says. With his thumb, he cocks the hammer. He feels solid now, more alive than he has in weeks.

"Jesus, kid!"

"Like it? My old man got it after you shot him." Polk holds the pistol sideways to show him. "Every week I'd go check in his shop where he hid it. I kept telling myself he was biding time, that any day he'd collect his payback."

The lawyer stares at the pistol. "He wasn't like that," he says. Then he calls again, "Louise!" her name a bark this time. "Call Tate."

"Sometimes a fantasy helps a man keep going," Polk says. He sidles around until he can see Embry and the back door, too. "A handgun hidden away, or a bottle, or maybe a woman he sees on the side."

"You got children?" Embry asks. "They change things, how things look."

Polk starts to tell him to shut up about that, intends to say that he isn't here to talk about kids. Before he can, the back door bangs open. He turns to look. A round-faced woman in a pink housecoat comes onto the porch. She's aiming a shotgun his way. "Louise, no!" Embry yells. "Get back inside."

As Polk's pistol comes up, a pain stabs deep in his right side. He grabs at the place, and his hand feels an inch of fletching and the shaft end. The sound of a shotgun blast shatters the air, shakes him bone deep. He ducks belatedly and rolls onto his side, the stab deeper now, rolls once to a kneeling stance. He raises the .38, all adrenaline now, as the shotgun clatters over the railing and pinwheels down to the ground. The woman lets loose a horrified scream and crumples to her knees.

Embry moves toward his wife. "Hold it!" Polk yells. Embry slows, his hands wide out to his sides and empty. Polk feels the blood on him now, a warm trickle inside his shirt from the crossbow dart. The shotgun blast, he's pretty sure, missed him entirely.

At the porch steps now, Embry takes a slow step up. "I said hold it," Polk says. He raises the .38, aims, and fires. The slug splinters the railing ahead of the man's hand. The lawyer stumbles back against the bright house. A burnt cordite smell etches the air. It stings and dries Polk's eyes.

"My wife," Embry says. "Please. She's no part of this."

With his free hand, Polk opens his shirt. His fingers find the dart's notched end and grip it. He pulls, feels it budge, slide out an inch. His blood flows more freely now, pulsing deep red around the yellow-fletched shaft. He presses a hand over the wound to slow the flow. A taste like new pennies fills his mouth.

"Think this through —," Embry says.

"Over there." Polk waves the pistol, indicating the corner of the house. His wound burns now, as if probed by a blacksmith's cherry-hot poker. A dizzy confusion fills his brain. This isn't how he wanted things to go, isn't how he planned. It's all messy now, noisy with the woman's wailing, pulsing with pain. Morning sunlight reflects from the white siding, unbearably bright, harsh behind his squinting eyes.

Embry moves back along the house, his hands out to shield his face. "Please," he says. "Oh God! Please."

Ten feet from the man, Polk raises the pistol. He brings his left hand, sticky with blood, up to the butt and steadies his aim. He draws a deep breath and holds it, squinting against the glare. "No," the man says, and then he repeats the word, keeps repeating it like an incantation. Polk tells himself he's done this before, for God's sake, killed total strangers in that place of silent, shimmering green. He can kill this man now, this Arnel Embry, this man who first poisoned their lives.

Seconds pass, ten, twenty. A rumble like a freight train fills his body. His breath comes out ragged and wet. Toby Polk, fevered and trembling now, tries but still he can't bring himself to squeeze, can't make himself do this one simple thing.

Squirrels

"There are squirrels in our attic," his ex-wife says. She's called his cell number. Rarely does she call the house phone, now that he's remarried. She hangs up if his new wife answers, denies, when he asks, that she ever called.

She never bothers with hello, doesn't say who she is, just starts in as though they talked yesterday. They didn't, though. They haven't talked for almost nine weeks. And they haven't seen each other in five years, not since their court date, things between them made final then, untangled and legally done.

The house still binds them, though. It's a grand house, suburban, big yard, lots of bedrooms upstairs for the kids they never had. She lives there. She'll tell anyone who cares to listen that she got the house, that he pays every month for his freedom — mortgage, taxes, and insurance. That's her version. He'll say she didn't get the house, not really. They own it together, an investment, fifty-fifty. She's just there until she finds another husband. Or seven years, whichever comes first. Then they sell. He's got it down on paper, signed and notarized. Irrefutable.

"You hear me?" she asks.

He strains to retrieve her words. "Squirrels? In the attic?"

"Every night they wake me up, playing up there, tumbling around. Or whatever it is they're doing. Breeding, maybe."

His ex-wife is not athletic. Two steps up a ladder and she's dizzy. There's no way she can shoo the squirrels out, no way she can patch whatever hole they come through.

"Call an exterminator," he says.

"I couldn't," she says. "No, I keep a broom beside the bed, jab the ceiling with the handle. That shuts them up, and I can sleep."

"Call," he says. "They'll nest up there."

"My tires need replacing," she says. "They've got tread wires poking out. The engine light blinks on at stop signs." Things have not been easy lately. He needs to understand. "And you're telling me to pay someone to catch squirrels?"

He doubts the part about her car. It has the scent of lies, ones he's heard before. Still, he'll use the opening. "Maybe we should sell the place," he suggests, not the first time. "Get our equity out."

"You'd want that, me stuck in some dinky apartment?"

"We're selling anyway," he reminds her, "in another two years."

"Where would I go?" Her question is rhetorical. She doesn't expect an answer, and he doesn't have one. "It's not fair," she mutters, "none of this."

He finds it incredible that, approaching forty, the woman still expects fairness in this life. He outgrew that years ago. It isn't the kind of thing he can tell her, though. It's not what she wants to hear.

He says, "The town must have an animal control officer?"

"They're not so bad, the squirrels." Her voice is softer now. "When it's quiet here, they're company."

"They're rodents," he says. "They gnaw wiring, chew the insulation off."

"The dining room light did quit working," she tells him, even though she's sure that started before the squirrels came.

"Bare wires can short out, spark, set the place on fire."

"These squirrels won't gnaw wires," she says. "They've got plenty of nuts out back, acorns and all. Don't worry so much."

He feels the old frustrations grow. "Listen," he says, as plainly as he knows how, "you have to get those squirrels out."

"Somehow they pried loose an attic vent," she says, as if she doesn't hear, "the one above our bedroom window. I watch from the deck, see them come and go from a hole up under the soffit."

Soffit — the word unsettles him. He wonders where she learned it, if maybe she's met a carpenter.

"They grab the gutter, swing up under, catch onto the opening, the pink insulation hanging out, and scramble in, their tails all jerky for balance. Every time, I hold my breath."

He feels a slow seething inside. "You just watch?"

"You'd be amazed." In that moment, inspiration arrives. She'll borrow a camera, make a videotape of the furry little acrobats, mail it to him, a surprise.

His head hurts. The woman has no idea what these animals can do. "They'll get trapped in your walls and die there," he tells her. "The stench will drive you to a motel, keep you there for weeks."

A motel? How arrogant! "I cannot afford a motel," she sputters.

"I'm saying the house will stink."

"Then I'll spray Lysol," she says, "or floral Glade. No one visits anyway."

"Listen. You remember when that mouse died in the kitchen wall, how long the smell hung on?"

Her laugh is a bright explosion. "Your brother and his wife — "

"Okay!" he interrupts. "Squirrels are ten times bigger than mice. Twenty times, maybe. The stink will last forever."

"I'll be fine." She feels scolded, hurt. "Don't worry."

"You can't . . . " Words fail.

"It's really not so bad," she says. To tell the truth, some nights she lies and listens, imagines what it must be like, romping in some stranger's attic, tumbling around up there until you get tired.

"I'll mail a check," he says. "You call an exterminator."

She imagines poison, leg-jaw traps, guns. "I couldn't."

"He won't hurt them. He'll relocate them, take them someplace with trees."

"They've got lots of trees," she says, "right out back. You remember."

He does remember—the trees, the yard, the two of them working back there in early summer heat—digging roots, piling rocks, planting seeds. "I'll send money," he says hoarsely, his throat a knotted sock.

"Okay," she says. "If you want."

"Okay," he echoes, eager now to hang up.

Her hand curls around the phone mouthpiece, cups it like a fat plastic ear. "Don't be mad, though," she whispers, "if I keep the squirrels for a while, if I buy tires instead."

Things Kept

Sometimes LeAnn felt restless, strange to her own skin. It was a troublesome feeling, one that would come on her without warning, as it did one Tuesday afternoon in late October. Her sister, Cass, had phoned. She had insisted that LeAnn drive down from Dayton and meet her at Panda's, a new coffee shop just off the interstate. Cass being Cass, she'd given no reason, not one hint of why. Sitting across the table from her now, LeAnn nudged last crumbs of rhubarb torte across her plate with the tines of a jittery fork. It wasn't helping her nerves one bit that Cass was hoarding her precious news. But it wasn't her sister's secrecy that made LeAnn feel so at odds with herself, and it wasn't the long drive down either. It was finding herself in this place again, her skin steeped again in its mocha and cinnamon smells.

LeAnn was chattering, and she knew it, rattling on about her husband, Lonnie, saying anything to smother the uneasy feeling. As she got to the part where Lonnie tells his boss where to go and what to do once he gets there, Cass slapped the table so hard that silverware rattled. The buzz of nearby conversations vanished in one quick gasp.

"Slow down!" Cass said. "You talk like a Yankee on fire."

The room felt too small, too warm, the air heavy as syrup. Everyone in the place seemed to crowd toward them. LeAnn wondered what they must think, if anyone took them for sisters, mismatched as they were, Cass plump in her best country house-dress, Pentecostal hair piled high and stabbed through with bone combs, LeAnn in tasteful makeup, her body trim, clothes and hair stylish—an offhand kind of casual, she liked to think. She leaned across the table and whispered to Cass, "Next time you ask me down, remind me there's restrictions on my speaking speed."

Cass jabbed the air with her fork like a finger. "You've got to let a body get a word in wedgewise."

"Edgeways," LeAnn said.

"I'm the one wants to get a word in," Cass said. "Trust me, edgeways don't get it." That was the maddening thing about Cass. Always had been. Even wrong, she was right.

"Go ahead then." LeAnn folded her hands and rested the fist-ball on the table edge. "I'm listening, if you're finally ready to tell."

Cass gave a little huffing sound. "First off, you know how mulish Ma can be," she said, "when it comes to taking help."

"Better hungry than humbled," LeAnn said.

"Exactly," Cass said. "If it weren't for her bum knees these days, there'd be no doing for her."

The uneasiness inside LeAnn had settled now. She was regaining herself. "They're worse?" she asked.

Cass's quick glance stung like an accusation.

"Her letters," LeAnn said, "they're all about weather and garden."

"Her knees and weight, too," Cass said. "Both slow her down."

Autumn sunlight came between the blinds of the coffee shop window and landed as harsh stripes on the tabletop. A tight tremble climbed LeAnn's back like a deep winter chill. Two-handed, she clutched the mug, still warm with coffee.

"She refuses to use her cane," Cass said. "Manages somehow to get herself out of the house, down the hill, and across the creek bridge when she needs. Every Sunday morning, she's there beside the apple tree, studying her Bible, waiting on me to come take her to church."

LeAnn never thought of her mother that way. When, gazing out the window of her neat Dayton kitchen, she might happen to think of her living back here, she pictured the sturdy woman who'd raised three girls and three boys in a house parked halfway up a rugged hillside. She'd done most of the raising, children and vegetables, while their father was off railroading, often as far as Illinois, gone sometimes for weeks at a stretch. Back then, her size felt like strength. And that was how LeAnn remembered her.

She'd last seen her mother in the spring when she'd come back to Spivey for her father's funeral. Walking along the cemetery path, LeAnn had slowed her pace and shortened her stride to match her mother's lumbering gait. Her mother's voice had gone brittle—from grief, she supposed. Back at the house, when LeAnn sat on the frayed, broken-spring couch, she slid toward the sinkhole where her mother always sat. But even though LeAnn had seen her mother not long ago, had seen she was old and fleshy and hobbled, that image had faded quickly. The mother in LeAnn's memory was too sturdy, too deep-rooted, to be so easily replaced.

"Anyway," Cass said, pushing her coffee mug aside, "Lem Tate thought we should know. She's late with her taxes. She'll lose the place if she don't catch up by first of the year."

LeAnn straightened in her chair. "You know I love her, Cass, but you can't expect Lonnie and me to take her, what with our three kids."

"When the time comes," Cass said slowly, "I expect you to help with Ma, just a couple weeks now and then. I can take her in spells. As an everyday thing, she's bound to wear me out."

"I'm sorry, but there's no way Lonnie—"

Cass slapped the table again. "What I'm saying is, right now we need to help her stay in that house," she said. "Gabe and me can scrape up a couple hundred dollars. We were thinking maybe you and Lonnie could, too."

LeAnn drew a deep cleansing breath and slowly let it out. "Of course." Just last week she'd peeled the sticker off a new Visa card and used it at Lazarus, a few private purchases that Lonnie could never know about. He kept his secrets, and she kept hers, too. There must be a thousand left on the card's credit line. Less, maybe, taken as cash.

"Dale wants to kick in, too," Cass said. "Can't say how much help he'll be. The boy's paying off three cars, two of them already totaled." For sixteen years, their baby brother had driven the roads of Burkitt County like his personal Talladega. To support his automotive habit, he tended bar at Lucky Threes out on Highway 1839. And, when the weather suited, he'd hire himself out for roofing.

"He still drive that Buick?" LeAnn asked.

"Black Monte Carlo. Two years old. Rolled once." Cass gave a weary wave with her hand and added, "So far."

"Sure, let the kid help," LeAnn said. "You know Ma won't take our money."

Cass slid her plate and fork aside, clearing a path between them. She folded her napkin into tight triangles and sharpened the creases with a fingernail, keeping her eyes on her work. "You remember Dexter Chalk?"

LeAnn flinched. "I moved away, Cass," she said, "I didn't get a lobotomy."

"Think you can persuade him to do something?"

Hell, yes, she could. He might be a God-fearing man, but if LeAnn said the word, Dex Chalk would burn a church.

"Might be I could," LeAnn said. "Long as it's nothing too illegal or immoral." She wanted to say it evenly, but the uneasy feeling rushed back now. Her throat tightened, and the words rasped out. She was aware of the air, how it moved on her skin, of a hundred small sounds in the place, of the ribbon of warm amber sunlight that lay like silk on her hand, of an iridescent fly buzz-walking the rim of her mug. LeAnn smiled in spite of herself.

Sometimes she thinks of herself as music. A song by Bonnie Raitt, maybe, the kind you'd crank up loud driving fast going nowhere. Scarred. Torn and achy with desire. Not prissy, not one bit sweet. Raunchy and used. Music haunted by echoes of things she cannot name.

One mention of Dex Chalk's name, and LeAnn felt that way.

"Chalk & Lytle" were the names on the ornate sign hanging above the appliance store door. Over the years, rain had dripped from its rusted ironwork and stained the concrete sidewalk below. Anchoring bolts shed slow rust tears down the brick storefront.

Only the oldest folks in Spivey remembered Mr. Lytle, although the story of his gruesome end—he was beheaded on Main Street one sunny morning when a rigging cable snapped—had been told and retold by generations of Burkitt County schoolchildren.

On the other hand, everyone remembered the succession of Chalks referred to by the sign—first Big Wilbur, now shriveling away at the county rest home, and then Little Wilbur, who had grown to twice his father's size. In the past year, Little Wilbur had taken up golf full-time and, for the most part, left the running of the appliance business to his brighter son, Dexter. Along the storefront benches of downtown Spivey, there was some disagreement about whether the name on that sign still referred to Little Wilbur or if that honor had now passed to young Dexter Chalk.

LeAnn stepped around the sidewalk rust stain as if it were something solid, as if she might stumble over it. She paused in front of the plate-glass display window. A passerby might think she was considering an appliance purchase. In fact, she was checking her reflection.

Not bad, she thought. She poofed her hair with her fingers and swung sideways to check for belly bulge. Nope, pancake flat. Fifty crunches in the morning and fifty more at night could do that. Cass could take a lesson from her.

LeAnn wet her lips, pulled the door open, and stepped inside. Dex Chalk was in the refrigerator aisle near the back of the store.

Wild black hair—he still wore his high-school hairstyle—overhung the collar of his pale blue shirt. He was talking business to someone, a delivery driver or installer, someone shorter than an upright freezer. Dex's voice sounded harsh as spilled tacks. It got that way sometimes, although never with her.

LeAnn ambled down the television aisle. Dex's head turned her way. "Be with you in a minute, ma'am," he said. "Feel free to look around. We got some beauties."

LeAnn felt a rush of rage at being called "ma'am." She was never called that in Dayton, and most surely she had never been called that by Dex Chalk.

He hadn't recognized her. That seemed certain. But now, as he talked business behind the freezers, his voice quieted and it took on a crooning quality, its sharp edges dulled as if there were a customer walking his showroom floor.

Before her, a hypnotic array of duplicate TV commercials advertised a pill that made you want to dance through weeds. LeAnn's throat felt parched. The store's air seemed to crackle with the static of stacked electronics. She sneezed.

Three aisles over, Dex Chalk turned and stretched to his full height. His smile flashed now, his boyish smile, the one she adored, and he waved his clipboard at her.

Good Lord, she thought. He recognizes my sneeze.

She sneezed again.

When she felt a third one coming on, she rushed toward the back of the store, toward his office. He kept a box of tissues on the corner of his desk. At least, he had last spring when he led her there by the hand, led her through the empty store, insisting she come see his office. He'd asked her to meet him later that evening at Panda's. And she did meet him there in that place rich with mocha and cinnamon smells, met him just for coffee and conversation, or so she told herself. Later that night they made love at an inn overlooking Norris Lake. Since then, she and Dex had secretly met five times—twice in Somerset, twice in Lexington, and once south of Cincinnati.

LeAnn knew Dex wouldn't like it, her going into his office all familiar-like. Spivey people loved to talk, after all. Someone might suspect. She opened his office door anyway and slipped in.

In a perverse way, she craved Dex's anger. She enjoyed it because of *how* he got angry. Irked and sweetly wobbled. Mildly pissed, his face alive with contour furrows and crescent dimples that made him even more handsome.

Besides, Dex's anger was never real anger, not at all like her husband Lonnie's.

LeAnn pulled off Highway 1839 and parked in the gravel lot beside Lucky Threes. Cass's Cutlass, their brother's once-rolled Monte Carlo, and a dinged and rust-pocked Ford pickup were the only other vehicles there. Dale had to work the afternoon shift behind the bar, so they'd had no choice about where to meet. This place was certainly near the bottom of LeAnn's list. Drinking among strange men gave her the willies.

"Took long enough," Cass said, as LeAnn climbed onto the stool beside her. The place was nearly empty, which suited LeAnn just fine. Cass snubbed out a half-smoked cigarette and waved her smoke away, a courtesy to LeAnn, who'd quit eight years ago.

"Don't mind me," LeAnn said to Cass. "Smoke if you want."

"Heineken?" Dale asked from behind the bar. Before LeAnn could answer, he slid the emerald bottle, its cap already popped, across to her. Foam erupted and streamed down the neck.

"The kid don't pour for his customers." Cass sipped a cold drink, an Ale-8-One.

"Only if there's a tip in it." Dale's face looked harder than LeAnn remembered, its angles sharper. He lifted her bottle to wipe the spill with his bar rag, and she caught sight of a metal stud the size of Delaware punctured through his left earlobe. LeAnn reached to touch it, and he leaned toward her.

"Is that thing permanent?" she asked.

Dale jerked back. "Damn! She's morphed into Ma."

"Bet you don't wear that round her," LeAnn said.

"Wears it inside his pants pocket," Cass said. "No lie. When he comes to see Ma, don't matter if it's a hundred degrees, Dale here is wearing long sleeves so she don't see them tattoos he's got drawed on his arms."

"Look who's talking," Dale said. "Church-girl keeps them cigarettes hid around her." He wiped his way down the bar and refilled the glasses of the two men seated there.

Cass tapped another cigarette from her pack, lit it, and inhaled deeply. "I'm working on quitting these things," she said, smoke floating out of her. "Been praying on it. It's just real hard right now." She pressed the cigarette into an ashtray slot and slid both down the bar.

"We all got our crosses," LeAnn said. She sipped her beer. Behind her nose, she felt the foam's tiny alcohol tickle. She decided she liked meeting here after all, the place nearly empty at this hour.

Dale came back and tossed the rag against the mirror behind the bar. He picked up Cass's cigarette, took a drag, and then replaced it and shoved the ashtray farther away. "So what's the word, Sis?" he asked, the smile crooked on his face. "Dex Chalk still got the hots for you?"

LeAnn slapped at him, even though he was out of reach. "Grow up," she said. That kind of thought she didn't want running through her kid brother's mind.

"He say he'll do it?" Cass asked.

"Can't," LeAnn said. "Little Wilbur still checks the books and counts cash. He'd never stand for buying merchandise back at more than a dime on the dollar."

"You saw the receipt," Cass said. "Daddy paid him better than eight hundred for that wide-screen TV just last Christmas. And we'd make up the cash difference from new, as long as Ma don't know where it come from. You tell Dex that?"

"If it was his to decide," LeAnn said, "Dex would do it in a heartbeat."

Dale retrieved the exiled cigarette. "We're dead then?"

"Not by a long shot," LeAnn said. "We got plan B." She plucked the cigarette from her brother's fingers and took a long, slow drag. The tobacco smoke nipped at her tongue, her throat, more delicious than she remembered. She felt herself float a little. As she watched in the mirror, smoke snaked from her mouth and drifted up.

"Good Lord, LeAnn," Cass said. "Ain't you just full of yourself?"

LeAnn's reflection looked out through a veil of smoke.

"And plan B is . . . ?" Dale asked when she'd stretched the silence too long.

"The desk."

Two puzzled faces stared at her.

"In the basement. The old rolltop out of Piney Bluff railroad station. The one Daddy used for his fly tying, wood carving, and what all. Dex remembered seeing it down there when he delivered the monster TV. Told me he tried to buy it off Daddy that very day."

"That old thing?" Dale said. "It's all gouged up, and the rolltop hangs in the track. Dex know it's broke?"

LeAnn sipped her beer and savored the moment. "He says there's a man down in Knoxville who'd give an easy thousand for it. Maybe more. Dex would have to charge Ma a hundred to haul it. That's enough to keep Little Wilbur off his back."

One by one, Dale popped the knuckles on his right hand. It was his way of thinking. Then he did the same with his left. Inside LeAnn, each snap felt like a rib cracking. After a second trip around his knuckles, Dale said, "And we don't have to slip him something extra?"

"What I'm thinking," LeAnn said, "is we kick in, say, a hundred each. Dex tells Ma that he got thirteen hundred for the desk, takes his hundred, and gives her twelve. That should cover back taxes and leave her with pin money."

"And if Dex gets more for the desk . . . ?" Dale asked.

"Gravy."

LeAnn had to drive fast, uncomfortably fast, to keep up with Cass's Cutlass. The pavement seemed too narrow, the curves too sharp, the ditches too deep and hugged close on both sides. Coal trucks, loud and perilously wide, raced past in the opposite lane, briefly blocking the sun. After a couple miles, she slowed and let Cass race ahead. In all, her drive from Lucky Threes to the home place on Colton Ridge Road would take fifteen minutes. To LeAnn it felt like going back twenty years.

A quick panic gripped LeAnn when, still a half mile from the house, she saw smoke rise above the ridge. But the plume was tight and solid gray, and she knew it was not a house burning or a brushfire running wild. She guessed that the neighbors, the Hickses, were burning stumps or maybe limbs brought down by last spring's ice storm. As she rounded the last curve, she saw a blazing pile of deadwood to the west of her mother's house. Smoke swirled and pale ashes rose as if climbing an invisible chimney. In the woods behind the house, a pair of chain saws snarled at each other.

LeAnn steered her car onto the weedy pull-off and parked between Cass's car and a shiny black and chrome pickup that belonged to Donnie Hicks. He was Annie Hicks's older boy, the responsible one, the one who owned his own generator, a garden tiller, an electric log splitter, and several sharp chain saws.

Cass was waiting beside the footbridge over Brighty Creek. From there a path led up to the house. LeAnn hurried past the misshapen apple tree near the entrance to the bridge, giving it one quick glance. Most of its fruit lay rotting on the ground now, speckled tan and puckered and thick with tiny insects. But she remembered the taste of those apples in summer, the snap as her teeth punctured the green skin, the sour squirt biting into the flesh. She shuddered.

Cass crossed the plank footbridge, and LeAnn followed. The hollow ka-thump of hard soles on old lumber echoed below. On the far side, LeAnn paused and looked back across the creek. Then she followed Cass up the winding path toward the house.

The house was shaped like a shoebox and sided in gray vinyl. It perched atop a tall foundation. The front door, never used, stood a full story above the ground. Everyone used the side door, which was reached by climbing a rock-paved slope beside the house. From that side, a narrow porch wrapped around and across the front. The downhill side of the foundation was completely exposed, every attempt at plantings in the shaded rock and clay soil having failed. The only interruption in the expanse of clay-spattered concrete was a sliding glass door, the kind that ought to lead onto a deck. Instead it led, one giant step down, to sparse grass tufts and hardscrabble lawn.

LeAnn shaded her eyes. "Jeez, the place looks run-down."

"You say that ever time."

"Well it's true. Looks smaller, too."

They were in the yard, Cass walking beside her now. "I guarantee it ain't shrunk."

"How'd we all fit, all eight of us, three tiny bedrooms, only one bath?"

"It's all we knew," Cass said. As if that answered anything.

"Listen," LeAnn said. "When we get inside, let me do the talking."

Cass stopped, grabbed her arm. "You be sure to come to it sideways, not all suddenlike. She's prideful as ever."

The chain saws were louder now, angrier. LeAnn's temples tensed, but she kept her words calm. "It's not like I don't know the woman."

"I'm just saying she gets touchy. Talk weather first. And when you do come to it, make like it was Dex thought the whole business up." Cass poked a stray strand of hair back into the stack on her head, made a new stab with the comb, and swiped the front of her dress with her hands.

"Okay," LeAnn said. "Let's go."

"Hello in the house," Cass hollered as they came around the side. No answer. At the door, she knocked, but the saws roared louder, and so she opened the door and went inside. LeAnn, feeling strangely like an intruder, followed.

In the front room, their mother, Georgia Selby, sat sewing at her machine. The rickety clatter and whir of its mechanism sounded as familiar as an old friend's voice to LeAnn. Now and then, her mother would help with piecework, hems and zippers mostly, that Annie Hicks brought home from her job at Tiny Togs. On a radio beside her, Gold City sang praise hymns, the volume raised in holy battle with the noise outside. An orange tabby cat lay curled at her feet.

LeAnn rapped a hard knuckle on the door casing. "Hey, Mama," she called.

"Will you look what the cat drug in!" The old woman levered herself to her feet and surrounded LeAnn in a hug that smelled like pie spice. "Let me look at you, child."

LeAnn stepped back and twirled a girlish pirouette.

"Why, look at them bones. You been ailing, LeAnn Marie?"

"Been dieting, Mama. I weigh exactly what I should."

The old woman untied her apron and tossed it across a box of toddler clothes. With flustered hands, she brushed her housedress straight. "I'd have wore something decent if you'd let me know you was coming."

"Spur of the moment," LeAnn said. "Anyways, you look fine."

"You bring me my sweet grandbabies?" she asked. "And where's that ornery husband of yours?" Her mother had seen Lonnie's temper up close. LeAnn wished her mother could see the boy in the man, too, that she could see him humbled and hurt sometimes and sweet the way he could be. Maybe then she wouldn't be so set against him.

"Left them back home, " LeAnn said.

"You come in the kitchen with me," Georgia Selby said. "There's fruit pies cooling for Donnie Hicks and that poor Wesley Chalk. They're busy out back just now. Won't mind, I'm sure, if you chunk yourself off a piece. You need it more than them boys do. Cassandra, you come along and have some, too."

At birth, poor Wesley Chalk's name almost certainly did not include "poor." But folks always called him "that poor Wesley Chalk." Not to his face, of course. In school, the boy never caught on to reading, and that slowed his progress. At fourteen, Wesley failed fifth grade, while his ten-year-old brother Dexter skipped ahead to grade six. That was when Little Wilbur decided his oldest son's future lay in outdoor work. Twenty-five years later, poor Wesley Chalk was the broad-backed helper everyone called when stumps needed pulling, when rocks needed hauling, or when there were downed trees to clear away.

LeAnn cut a sliver of pie for herself, flopped it onto a knobby glass plate, and gave the knife to Cass. Their mother filled the coffeepot and set it to brew.

LeAnn fished a fork from the drawer. "How's your garden?"

"That mess? Thank the Lord it's out back where folks can't see." She eased herself onto a chrome-framed chair. It creaked and canted slightly as it caught her weight and settled.

"Wasn't a good year, was it, Mama?" Cass said.

"Sorriest garden I ever raised. Beginning of June, I was laid up a week and the weeds took over."

"They can do that," Cass said.

"It's untelling. Should've called Donnie Hicks right then, told him to come till it under. Would've saved me the shame of seeing it ever day."

"Wasn't your fault," Cass said, "knees acting up like they did."

"Not saying it's a fault, child. But if a body keeps a garden, they're obliged to see it comes to something." Her preacher eyes shifted from Cass to LeAnn and back again.

The pie tasted tart to LeAnn, as though her mother had shorted the sugar. She set her fork down. "Weather's terrible dry up north," she said. Cass gave her a quick nod.

"Rained plenty here," Georgia said, "else I wouldn't let them boys burn fires. You remember the time your father—God rest— accidental lit up the hillside. That blaze ran straight up the north ridge. Praise Lord, the wind blowed right, else we'd have lost the house."

This story, which dated from before LeAnn's birth, was the one her mother always told whenever brushfires or dry weather came up in conversation. In recent years, that old blaze had grown larger, spread farther, and come even nearer the house.

Cass said, "LeAnn was telling me she ran into Dexter Chalk this morning. You'll never guess." She turned toward LeAnn. "But you tell it."

Taken by surprise, LeAnn coughed, cleared her throat, and poured a glass of water for herself while she stitched together the tale. "Right," she said. "Anyways, I had lunch with Cass, and afterwards I was looking at portable TVs over at Chalk & Lytle, because I was thinking maybe Lonnie'd like one out in the garage, and who comes up and starts talking to me but Dexter Chalk."

Her mother's eyes brightened. "He still sweet on you?"

"It's been years."

"Broke his heart, you did." Georgia pushed herself up from the chair. "He mooned over you forever when you moved away. Asked after you ever time we'd pass on the street. Folks said he'd never get married."

LeAnn forged ahead. "What he talked about is wanting to buy Daddy's old desk."

"Downstairs," Cass added quickly. "The rolltop one come out of Piney Bluff Station. Dex seen it once and remembered."

"That old thing? Whatever . . . ?"

"Don't know how much to believe," LeAnn said, "but he claims this man in Knoxville gives twelve hundred cash money, maybe more, for a desk like Daddy's."

A troubled look shaded Georgia's face as she sank back onto her chair. "Your father kept things in there, private things, old knives he wore out but couldn't bring hisself to pitch, Confederate money his people passed down, and Lord knows what else. They was things important to him."

Cass patted her mother's thick shoulder. "You said you went through his stuff."

"Upstairs things. Wasn't no rush on the other."

"You haven't gone through the desk?" LeAnn asked.

"Touched nothing down there. Them stairs is too steep for me. Besides, he always kept the outside slider door braced with a broom handle."

"I'll run down and unlock it," Cass said. She hurried toward the basement door. "You two come around the outside, and I'll let you in."

"No!" The old woman's voice was April thunder. Cass, already halfway down the steps, might have heard. If she did, she did not stop.

"Grab a jacket and come," LeAnn said.

"We got no right rummaging down there," Georgia said. "Your father wouldn't want it." But even as she protested, she shuffled to the peg beside the door where her gardening sweater hung.

"It's all right," LeAnn said. "It'll be all right." She held the door open for her mother. Once on the side porch, she offered an arm for balance. Awkwardly attached, they negotiated the plank steps to the ground and worked their way down the side slope.

As they stepped over the drainpipe at the corner of the foundation, the glass door slid open with a series of gritty, rusty squeaks. Cass leaned out.

Inside, the air felt like damp linen against LeAnn's skin. Her eyes gradually adjusted to the dim light that came from the room's only lamp. She didn't know this room, not in the way she knew those upstairs. Back then, this had been a place of unfinished rafters and bare concrete, a place for outgrown clothes and things broken but too good to toss. One thing was constant though. Then, as now, in the far corner sat their father's railroad desk.

When Harlan Selby retired, all the basement junk got pitched. After he paneled the walls and wired baseboard heat, their father lugged down his easy chair, a few sticks of furniture, a favorite lamp—a black ceramic panther lamp salvaged from an L&N train wreck—and he had himself a den. The first TV was a used portable. Everyone on it had orange faces. Then came a new nineteen-inch, then two years ago a satellite dish, and this past Christmas the monster TV.

LeAnn came around the couch. Something brushed her face, a cobweb, she guessed. Dust sizzled up from the lightbulb, bright as party sparklers. Beside the lamp, a cigar stub balanced on the lip of a lily-pad ashtray. With her index finger, LeAnn toppled it into the ashes. As her hand skimmed past a dusty beer bottle, a spider retreated over the bottle lip and back into the amber glass neck.

Near the door, the old woman fidgeted. She hugged her sweater tight across her chest as if she'd trapped something wild inside. LeAnn walked to the dark monster TV. She traced a finger across its dust-covered screen. "How you must have hated this thing," she said.

"What do you know about it?" There was gristle in Georgia Selby's voice now as she came close. She wiped her sleeve across the screen. "This is the last thing I ever bought Harlan," she said, "excepting his grave rock. I must have sewed six thousand zippers last fall so he'd have it for Christmas."

"Come look here," Cass called from the back of the room. Somehow she'd gotten the rolltop open. LeAnn came closer. Balanced in her sister's hand was a wood carving, a tiny steam locomotive.

"That one he carved the winter the union walked out," Georgia said, taking it. "John come that year, which makes it 1961." She could mark most years in that decade by a child just born or one about to be.

Cass stepped to one side. On a pile of wood chips sat a cherry block rough-gouged to a coal-car shape. At least it looked like a coal car to LeAnn. Three tiny chisels lay nearby. Cass swept the chips aside and peered into the desktop compartments. "Letter slots are filled with fishing stuff, flies and lures and such. We'll need better light," she said over her shoulder. "Get plastic bags for this stuff, too."

Their mother, the locomotive still cupped in her hands, had retreated to the light of the doorway. Her face was turned to the side, her head cocked. She seemed to be listening intently, but not to either of them.

LeAnn turned back to the desk. She tugged the brass knob of a shallow drawer running beneath the letter slots. It was locked. She picked up the smallest wood chisel and worked it in the keyhole, jiggled it around. The lock held fast.

"You stay out of that key-locked drawer. Your father kept papers in there, important things he meant kept private."

"You got the key?" LeAnn asked.

"You hear me? It's private."

"It's okay," Cass said. "We'll empty it into a shoebox for you, Ma. Won't take so much as a peek. Honest."

The old woman seemed to shrink. Her voice trembled. "The key, it was always in his pocket. Like as not, it's in the envelope now."

"What envelope?" LeAnn asked.

"I believe," she said, her voice sounding weak, "I put it in the Bible table drawer."

LeAnn took the stairs two at a time. In the front room, she pulled open the Bible table drawer. Inside, she found a large sealed envelope. Scrawled across it in careless black script—"Personal Effects, Harlan Selby." She slipped a fingernail under a corner of the flap. She intended to slit it, find that key, and take it to her mother. But a chill like death's breath brushed her cheek, and she drew her finger back. Instead, she carried the envelope, still sealed, down the stairs and handed it to her mother.

"Why?" LeAnn's question hung in her throat.

"I stuck it away and more or less forgot," Georgia said.

"Amen, Mama. Now open it," Cass urged.

Slowly, tenderly, the old woman worked open one flap edge and then tore the envelope seam. She winced as if ripping flesh. When it was open, she dumped the contents in a quick cascade. One wallet, brown, worn thin at the fold, twelve dollars inside; one small jackknife with a cracked pearly inlay; one pair nail clippers; one gold wedding band, worn thin; one silver pocket watch with chain;

two quarters and one nickel. And sliding out last, one ornate brass skeleton key.

LeAnn grabbed for it, but her mother snatched it up, squeezed it in her fist, and buried the fist in her sweater pocket. LeAnn extended her hand, and Georgia drew back. "Fetch a shoebox or a flour sack, Cassandra," LeAnn said. "We'll empty it for you, Ma."

"We shouldn't open it," the old woman said.

LeAnn reached for her mother's arm. "I'll help you get back upstairs. We'll take care of it. Everything goes in bags without us looking. Scout's honor."

"No," she said. Her voice had gone wispy now, like river reeds in a breeze. "He didn't know that day, didn't know he'd die fast. He just went for a haircut. There's no warning, no time to get things in order, set things like he'd want them found."

She was weakening, and Cass pushed ahead. "Go with LeAnn, Ma. We'll have it cleaned out and wiped down. By time Dex comes in the morning—"

The old woman stiffened. "What right have you got," she said, "what right behind my back telling Dexter Chalk he can have it?"

LeAnn flinched. "He'll pay you cash money for it, Ma. Cash money."

"I'm saying no. You stay away from his things."

"Think on it a minute," LeAnn said. "Just think. That desk is doing you no good. Lord knows, you'd find use for the money." She wanted to shout about unpaid taxes, wanted to invoke the name of Lem Tate. But she knew if she did, the battle was lost.

"I make do."

"But—," Cass began.

Georgia turned and shuffled to the doorway. "You've heard my last word on it. Now you girls had best let it drop."

"Old woman's a damned fool," Cass muttered as they reached the footbridge. "You want me to call Dex Chalk so he don't show up in the morning? Or do you want to tell him?"

"Neither."

Cass stopped on the bridge. "He's expecting the desk."

LeAnn leaned two-handed on the railing. "Think about it, Cass. Ma's afraid of what's in that drawer seeing light. Tonight, she'll ponder and pray on it. If I know her, she won't sleep at all. Before dawn, she's bound to realize it'll get opened someday soon. She's got no choice. It might be three months or it might be three years, but the day will come when she's hobbled so bad she can't manage out here."

"Or she's resting beside Daddy," Cass added.

"Or that," LeAnn said. "Either way, that desk will get opened soon enough. She's got no way around it. Give her a few hours and she'll see what's true. This time, her last word ain't law. In fact, last word don't belong to her at all."

"So we let Dex bring his truck out here in the morning?"

"I'm betting he'll drive away with that desk."

LeAnn had forgotten how, long after daybreak, the sun hung below Colton Ridge and mist fairies danced along Brighty Creek. She sat in her car and watched squirrels nudge acorns into the leafy banks. And she lit the seventh cigarette from her pack, a pack bought in the middle of the night from the lobby vending machine at the Somerset Oberlin Inn by a sweetly cautious Dexter Chalk. Bought for her, for LeAnn McCray, just because she asked him.

She opened the car door and stepped out. The morning air felt as brisk as first frost on her skin. She crossed the bridge, pausing to flip her half-smoked cigarette into the upstream side. She stayed long enough to watch the current carry it under the bridge, out the other side, and down through the first rocky rapids.

LeAnn started up the hill. A jaybird squawked, its sound a startling, angry scrape behind her eyes. Ahead, two smoke plumes rose from yesterday's fires—one faint, the other roiled with the fury of new fuel. She rounded a bend in the path, and the house came into view, its roof in bright sunshine, the side still shaded by the ridge. And shambling toward her with his swaying, muscle-bound gait came poor Wesley Chalk.

Wesley smiled broadly and tipped two fingers to the bill of his grubby green baseball cap. "Morning, LeAnn," he said. "Donnie come yet?"

"Didn't see him. You're here mighty early."

"I slept by the fires. Your ma, she worries they'll burn themselves loose. Me and Donnie, we're careful. I stayed anyways so she don't worry."

"Good to be careful." LeAnn inched away up the path.

"Lucky I stayed," Wesley said, following her now. "I come awake to see your ma hauling on this old-timey desk out front. She's pushing and shoving. But mostly she's just scuffing up rocks and dirt with it."

LeAnn's head went dizzy, her insides loose.

"She asks will I help lug it over to the side hill. Well, I do, and it is heavy, I should say. When we finally gets it there, she gives it a shove, and it tumbles down onto yesterday's fire. Sends sparks flying everwhere."

LeAnn turned unsteadily toward the crackling blaze. But it wasn't the old desk her eyes sought just then. It was Lonnie she looked for, Lonnie she expected to see tumbling over rocks, through the bright blaze, coming to his feet all scuffed and smudged, coming up grinning on the other side.

"Your ma paid me, too," Wesley said. "Paid better'n Donnie does." He pulled a fistful of money from his pocket. "See? Twelve dollars," he said, spreading the bills. "And two quarters and a buffalo nickel. She give me this old pearly-handle jackknife, too."

Sometimes she thinks of herself as a howl. The wail of a coyote, maybe, or a lone banshee, a shriek dying away in the night without reaching ears. Piercing, like something wrenched raw from an orphaned soul. A hollow thing, haunted, a sound that lives on, still shrill in memory long after its echo dies.

As she raced north toward Dayton that morning, LeAnn felt that way.

Paragon Tea

"Leave the cell phone," I tell Eli as we get out of his car.

He glares at me across the blue Corvette, the car I gave him on his twenty-first birthday. It's a convertible, perfect for L.A. His mother called it a death car. At first Eli said he wanted no part of it. A guilt offering, that's what he called it. He parked it behind his mother's garage in El Cajon, the red bow still tied across the hood, and drove his sun-faded Celica instead. Better gas mileage, that was his excuse. Stepping lightly in the world, he said. Living green. Now that I'm back from India, I see that he's driven the Corvette, though. Eighteen months I've been gone—back and forth, but mostly there—and he's driven it plenty. I checked the odometer getting in. Don't get me wrong. I'm glad he's finally using the car, getting some enjoyment from it, even if he has forgotten where it came from.

Eli reaches behind the seat, gathers up a tattered script, and hugs it to his chest. His hair is a toadstool cap on top, buzz-cut high up the back and sides. He regards me through dark-rimmed glasses, the lenses small, like almonds. He's still holding the cell phone, holding it like a hand grenade. The kid's considering options, I know, weighing old hurts again.

"Please," I say. "Just leave it."

His eyes are a cold brown. They try to tell me that I'm nobody, that I'm not his father, that, genetics be damned, he's not a Selby, too. My longtime business partner, Vijay, warned me this wouldn't be easy, meeting here on Eli's turf. I told Vijay this was no negotiation. To him, everything is.

The balance in Eli's brain must tilt in my favor, because he stows the phone in the car console. He slams the lid with a theatrical flourish and hands the keys to the restaurant parking valet, a baggy sack of attitude, all slouched and mostly untucked. As the kid speeds away, keys and all, I remember my luggage crammed into the trunk, the ornate silver Ganesha gods packed inside, gift-wrapped in gold foil for my wife, Jessica, who waits for me in our Kentucky house, and daughter, Alyssa, living now in Rhode Island. Those Ganeshas are unique, they're expensive, and they're ripe for pilfering.

On the drive in from LAX, Eli was placing calls and taking calls about this script of his. The production company is on the fence, he tells someone, but leaning. Yes, the project could be green-lighted, he confides, under some unnamed major studio's independent shingle. An agent's client wants a guarantee that she can test for the Mollie role, wants Eli's word on it.

Late-morning traffic on the 405 Freeway slows, congeals, the sun already white-hot. Yes, he's open to beefing up the role, he says, maybe grouping her second-act lines into a monologue, creating a story point of sorts. Yes, the part's small, but it's meaty. Pivotal. *Gravitas*, he says, seeming to savor the word in his throat and mouth.

We start moving in traffic again, exhaust fumes drifting past us. He's thinking, he says, that it needs someone special, a young Teri Garr, someone authentic who will truly inhabit the role. Yes, he tells a caller, he's heard rumors of interest from other actresses, although he can't imagine how word got out. The production company is trying to fly this project below radar. Inside, I feel a kind of pride. This boy of mine, how good he is at verbal dance, how good at the game Vijay calls "always-open doors," at never saying no.

At the restaurant now, Los Angelinos Cantina, the maître d' greets Eli by name. He seats us on the patio beneath a white umbrella printed with pastel tropical fruit—halved mangoes, guava, sliced kiwi fruit. In the midday breeze, the fabric skirt makes small snapping sounds. On the patio blocks, its shadow flutters, birdlike beside our shoes.

Eli drops his script on the rippled glass tabletop and weights the flailing pages with a bowl candle. He checks his watch, then looks away, looks past me, his glance flitting across other faces in the place.

"So, how's the plant-closing business, Peter?" he asks. "Flourishing?" He wants to get into it, get it over with. Eli hates what I do, which is to say what I did, hates my business, hates the whole globalization thing. In high school, he'd send clippings to my Somerset office. He mailed them anonymously, articles about plant closings and layoffs, juvenile epithets scrawled in the margins. The El Cajon postmarks were dead giveaways. He tries to mask it now, his animosity, but it still burns in his eyes. I'm good at what I do, and maybe that's what irks him so. Or maybe it's that I don't apologize.

"Business? Tiring," I answer truthfully, and I manage to smile. My brain is fogged, still lagged from the flight. Lately, I'm feeling older than my forty-five years. A little burned out—that's what Vijay called it as he poured me a farewell whiskey. Why should I get into it with Eli now, the whole business with Global Solutions, Inc.? It's in the past anyway.

"So . . . Delhi?" He says it the way he'd say Denver or Dallas, just another place.

"Bangalore." Saying the name transports me to the place I've just left. "India's huge. Hard to get a handle on it all," I say. "The size of the place, people everywhere."

He waves to a halter-topped waitress, who clomps over on blocky-soled shoes. Her bright butterscotch hair shoots up in two fountainlike sprays. "I'll have a Gruyére croissant, Daphne," Eli says. "Paragon tea over crushed ice and a wheat-grass chaser."

"Would you like a menu?" Daphne asks me. She's not carrying one. Her voice is breathy, her diction precise. I'm guessing she takes me for a producer, a director, a casting god of some sort. My order, a BLT and Coke, seems to disappoint her.

Eli's fingers drum the tabletop, eight fingertips, two thumb knuckles tapping out his coded impatience. "So," he says. "No limo this time?"

"They have this smell," I say. "Vacuum-cleaner exhaust spiked with lemon." Smells that I hardly noticed before bother me lately. I worry that it's a sign of something.

His gaze visits other tables.

"You ski this year?" I ask. "Aspen? Vail?"

"You're kidding," he says. "I haven't skied since that time you took me, and it rained. I was what? Fourteen?"

"We should go," I say. "Skiing. Just the two of us. Rent a cabin for the week."

"I'm in the middle of things, Peter," he says. "My spec script and all."

He's two years out of film school. It'll be his first script sale, if it happens, his first movie. Quietly, I've done what I can. Not *all* I can, but enough. Lately I've been thinking about harmony, about the order of things, butterfly disturbances, cosmic ripples in the universe. If my kid's got what it takes, he'll find his intended place without boosts from me. Still, I worry that he's too naive, that he lacks the savvy he'll need to close the deal.

Daphne brings our drinks. A mint sprig garnish floats in my Coke.

"Let's plan on Aspen," I say, taking out my scheduler, leafing ahead to empty pages. "What do you say? I hear the new trails—"

"You don't come around for years at a time. I'm supposed to drop everything?"

"I've been busy," I say. "You understand busy." It sounds

harsher than I intend. Confrontational. Not a good tone for us, especially now. I breathe in, hold it, drain the tension, and find my calm center again. I breathe out.

"My mistake." Eli reaches for his script and stands. "I thought maybe—"

"Wait!" I grab for his hand, catch his wrist. "I know this is hard."

"I don't know what you expect."

"Sit," I tell him, catching my tone again, bringing it down. "Please sit. Drink whatever that is."

"Paragon tea," he says, like it's a normal thing and I should know.

"Listen, Eli. I've got something . . . I want you to hear this from me."

He does sit, on the edge of the chair this time. He plucks the straw from his drink, tosses it on the table, lifts the glass to his lips, and gulps. The straw leaks a small tea puddle onto the table. Beneath it, his knees start a nervous jitter-dance. "Say away." He glances at his watch again. "I'm meeting some people in Sherman Oaks in a little while."

"You can't give me a couple hours?"

He sits back now. "Next time call ahead, Peter, let me know you're coming. And that doesn't mean a call from the airport."

"I didn't know I was coming. After India, the plan was to lay over in Hawaii for a few days, get a tan, walk the beach. It was rainy, though, when my flight landed."

The way he looks at me, I know he's not buying it. The thing is, it's true. Mostly true anyway, which is to say nothing is provably false. It's just what I'm leaving out, the drinks in the airport bar with the *Wall Street Journal* reporter, how I let the news about Global Solutions slip, so unlike the old me. It'll be in the *Journal* tomorrow. The *L.A. Times*, too, no doubt.

"So it was raining in Honolulu," he prompts.

"Right," I say. "I see this flight to L.A. loading, and I think, what the hell."

"Ah," he says, as if he suddenly understands. "I'm some passing thought? Is that it? What the hell, it's raining, I'll go look up that kid, you know, the one I fathered on Malibu Beach back in '78?" His mother's told him everything. Carol's always been like that, so open the wind blows straight through her. Transparent.

Why that woman thought she'd make it as an actress, I'll never understand. She's an illustrator now, living in El Cajon, a much better fit.

"You know I don't mean it that way," I say. "It's more like, what the hell am I doing here when I could be getting reacquainted with my son?" My gaze is steady, returning his, and it occurs to me how much looking at Eli is like looking into a time mirror, seeing my earlier self there.

"Reacquainted?" He looks away. "We don't qualify for reacquainting. There's a prerequisite. We'd have to actually *acquaint* first. Twelve days in twenty-four years doesn't do it."

Carol doesn't like me coming around, doesn't want me influencing the kid. Surely he knows that. He must. I stir my straw through the ice-choked Coke, swirl it until the mint sprig sinks beneath an iceberg.

Daphne brings our plates and slides them in front of us.

Eli rips his croissant apart and takes a hurried bite. I remember what he said about meeting people in Sherman Oaks.

I pull toothpicks from my BLT and draw a deep breath. "You know my company?"

He looks up from his croissant. "Final Solutions?"

"Not funny." I resist the urge to defend Global's business one last time.

"Irreverent, maybe? Cynical? Edgy? That's what I was shooting for."

"Save it for the movies, Eli," I say.

He shoves the plate away, starts to stand. "I don't know why—"

"I got out," I say to stop him.

He stares, sits, his expression uncomprehending.

"What I'm trying to tell you, what you'll probably read in the newspapers tomorrow, is that I sold my half of the business to Vijay." Twenty-eight million, I want to tell him, want to see his face. But I don't. I can't make myself.

"You sold Global Solutions?" Eli leans toward me. "Damn! I thought you got off on all that, the power, all those stuffed suits sucking up, traveling everywhere, hawking your balance-sheet snake oil."

"Is it me you hate?" I ask.

He doesn't answer.

"I thought maybe it was my business, that you had some aversion to the whole outsourcing thing."

"And a week in Aspen will fix everything?"

"I'm trying—"

"Go back to your family," he tells me. He means Jessica, our house in the Kentucky hills most of a continent away.

I ask, "What do you want from me?"

"Nothing. Not one goddamn thing."

Someone turns up L.A.'s volume. Diners yell across their tables now, shout into cell phones, into licorice-whip headsets. Cars accelerate and rumble by, radios pulsing windows. A windshield flares like a second sun. Heat dizzies my brain. I grasp my Coke, gulp some, then roll the glass, cold and slick, against my wrist.

On the table between us, Eli's hands lie flat as fish. His gaze meets mine, holds it. The glint in his eye is as familiar as yesterday. I reach across, pick up his straw, and dab the last drop of tea on my tongue. The taste is foreign, astringent, like nothing I'd ever drink.

Flights

"Unexpected gifts," whispers the plump nurse, whose name I've forgotten. "That's what remissions are."

From beneath his pillow, my father takes a photograph. It's black and white, small and square, the edges deckled in crisp half-moons. He taps the gloss image with his tough fingernail. "That's me," he says, showing it, "me and Betty Lowe."

It's Mom and Dad all right, so young in swimsuits.

He lies back on his bed. "I was twenty-two, Betty, seventeen. We picnicked, down on the river."

"You remember?"

The nurse pokes me. "Don't spook the gift," she seems to mean. The doctor warned, of course, that there'd be lucid days. "Keep your hopes in check," he reminds me again, clicking his pen like some code. "These brief remissions aren't significant in the longer view of things." He pockets the pen as he leaves.

"Everyone's gone now who cares," my father says. "Once I'm gone, it'll be like it never happened." There was more life in his eyes, more animation in his face than I'd seen in a very long time, and coherence to his words.

"I'll remember," I say. "I'll care."

"My son's a writer," he tells the nurse, as if I'm not there. "He can imagine anything, make it up from nothing, and care like it was real."

I turn away, scolded and shamed, still his boy at fifty-six.

"Here's a tablet," she says to me, "a felt-tipped pen."

I take them and a tissue that she offers, too. There's an Indian on the tablet cover, a chief in full headdress. Inside, the paper is pale, like old skin. The lines are the color of veins.

"Write this down," my father tells me, pointing. "All of it."

I uncap the pen, touch nib to paper. "A perfect day," I write, knowing that's how he'll begin.

"A perfect day," he says, "the river high on its banks. Chill water laps our ankles. Beneath our feet, river rocks are slippery with moss. There's a muddy smell to the breeze, and shore weeds make riffle sounds like pennants in stiff wind. Downriver, a paddle wheeler puffs out clouds of steam, its whistle shrill, louder than any toy."

I look over when he pauses. It's so good to see his face alive like this. As he starts up again, my breath catches high in my chest. It's all I can do to go back to writing.

"Betty's beside me, on the plaid blanket we've spread—three blankets, three couples, my box camera passed around. A Victrola somewhere plays music, Skinny Ennis singing 'Too Many Tears.' Overhead, split-tail martins fly cursively. We try to read their penmanship, decipher what they write on the undersides of clouds. Betty traces their paths with a weed stem she's plucked. 'Maybe,' she whispers close to my ear, 'they're writing infinities.'"

"Wait," I say, scrawling fast now. "Infinities?"

My father's eyes find me. "Like eights," he says. "Just write."

"Just write," the nurse says, too.

The old man sits straighter now in bed, propped on an elbow. "Betty tells me, 'Infinity means forever in algebra. Enormous. More than you can ever know.'"

I draw the symbol on my pad and he nods.

"I like that she's smart," he says, "don't get me wrong. But more it's how it feels right then, me beside her. Even before I touch her, I know how her skin will feel. And even before we kiss that first time, I know it'll be like something we've always done."

"I can't write that," I tell him. "It's sentimental slop."

"It's true."

"True don't count for shit," I say. "Give me specifics to write, not conceptual crap."

"Specifics?"

"Like the river stuff. That was good. Only this time about Mom."

"Okay." He's on his back now, not looking at the photo any-more. He watches the ceiling like a movie screen. "Auburn hair scrolled up on both sides. Ribbon-tied, a wisp loose at her neck. Her face is all soft curves. Not a straight angle anywhere, except the ridge of her nose. And freckles, God, a mask of freckles—pale so you only notice up close—under her eyes, across that gorgeous nose. Soft shoulders beneath her swimsuit straps. And her pulse like a metronome in the hollow of her neck. The rise and fall of her breathing is God's own lullaby."

It's the nurse who interrupts this time. "You miss Betty," she says. It seems obvious to me.

"Every day." He seems weary. "She died young. A quick cancer. Summer of '55."

"I miss her." I write it, say it out loud, and write it again and again.

The nurse comes close. Her smell is dry talcum. "You were . . . what? Six?"

"Six," I say. "I remember, though. Even more, I remember this photograph, the way my father brightened each time he brought it out. He needed me to know about that day, to care, to not let the memory die."

The nurse sits beside me on the bed. A slipper dangles from my toe, dangles but doesn't fall. "Can you remember," she asks, "the last time your father took that photo out and told about that day?"

It feels like a trick, this question. I know two answers, either one right. Both right. "Just now," I start to say. I slide the photo back under my pillow. "And 1972, October second, the day before he died."

"Lie back now on your bed," the nurse tells me. She eases the tablet from my hand. "We'll write more tomorrow."

"Don't let her," Father seems to whisper.

I grab it back.

"Write me alive," he says. "Write me confused in this hospital, rambling. Write a plump nurse at my bedside. Write that day down, son. Keep it alive, the river smell, the tattered blanket we spread, my Betty beside me, the stem of her weed tracing martin flights."

Things Left Behind

━━━━━━

1

Dex Chalk still lay in the motel bed ten minutes after LeAnn McCray had left. He wanted to remember everything about the past few hours so days and weeks from now, in his most private mind, he could relive every detail—the liquid look in her eyes as she looked at him, the quickening touch of her hands, her salty tang on his tongue, the pulse and pull of her urgency. As he lay there, though, the night's sensations faded, replaced by a growing dread of the long weeks ahead.

He threw back the covers, swung his legs over the side of the bed, and sat. In the dark, he could forget that the room was a rented one at Oberlin Inn, that the bed, the bland walls, the fake art framed and bolted there, that the locked-down TV and remote-on-a-rope must have witnessed the couplings of a hundred others. No, more. Thousands probably. Dex stood and pulled on his briefs. The pressure building in his skull felt like a bad bourbon hangover.

There had been no bourbon, of course. No booze of any kind. Not for one hundred eighty-seven days, counting today. And now that his feet had hit the floor, he did count today. *Abide within positive interpretations.* He'd culled that gem from a deck of affirmation cards belonging to his wife, Lovie, copying it into his sobriety journal.

He flipped the switch on the bathroom wall. The fluorescent light buzzed, flickered, and came on fully bright. The ceiling fan revved, then slowed, moaned, slipping octaves, its motor laboring. The plastic grate covering the fan rattled. The air, still tropical from LeAnn's shower, carried an acrid hint of cigarette smoke. Beside the sink in a plastic tumbler half-filled with water, three butts floated, filter end up. Dex lifted the tumbler and studied the tobacco-stained water, amber under fluorescents. It gleamed like cheap scotch. The old craving invaded him. It moistened his mouth and clawed at the back of his throat. He let himself believe that it was scotch. He could taste it on his tongue, could savor it warm and pure in his mouth. It filled him like sweet liquid music.

Dex growled, a low rumble, his voice reverberating deep in his chest. The growl was his thought stopper, a mind trick he'd read. Some people snapped rubber bands on their wrists. Others pinched the skin web between fingers to kill wrong thoughts. Dex growled. He liked how the sound scoured the illusion of taste from his throat, driving the cravings from his mind. He emptied the tumbler into the toilet, pissed into the mess, and flushed.

LeAnn had come back into his life on the second day of this, his third serious run at sobriety. It was the day of her father Harlan Selby's funeral, a day perfumed with budding spring shoots and moist earth smells. Dex had gone to the cemetery, unsteadily and mentally fogged, had gone to pay graveside respects. And maybe, he realized now, he'd gone seeking LeAnn and the young man he'd been with her.

In the months since that somber and tentative reunion, Dex had told LeAnn nothing about his drinking, about what it had made of him. In her eyes, he realized, he must still seem untarnished. And that was the way he wanted it. Drink was in his past now, anyway. Why bring it up?

LeAnn smoked. When had she taken that up? This created a certain problem for him. He'd have to lie to Lovie now. With her sensitive nose, she'd smell the smoke on his clothes before he opened the door.

"Oberlin Inn screwed up," he'd say, waving a hand carelessly. "Smoking rooms were all they had left. Checked in late. Car trouble. Nothing serious, dear." Then he'd kiss her forehead and she'd want to believe.

With a washcloth, Dex wiped a clear patch on the fogged mirror. His eyes—whites pure, blue irises bright as a child's—looked as they had before it all started. Clear eyes, clear mind. Who needs AA anyway? Not Dexter Chalk. True, there had been days early on when he wondered if he'd make it, when he wondered if the demons ever died. Well, he had made it, and he'd done it on his own. He deserved these moments of pride.

When Lovie checked his eyes, she'd find reassurance there. But she'd give him a breathalyzer kiss anyway. Who could blame her? She'd lived with his drinking so long. In a way, she'd survived it, too. When she smelled cigarette smoke, she'd suspect he'd stopped for a drink at Lucky Threes or some other roadside tavern. She wouldn't suspect he'd been unfaithful.

Unfaithful. How odd, that word. Odd, because he *had* faith now, faith for the first time in years, faith in himself, faith in a future beyond the next drink. In his rebirth, in these weeks of sobriety, LeAnn had played a large part. Maybe the largest one. Okay, strictly speaking, he had been unfaithful. But he had never been *more* faithful to his essential self, to his potential for good. Such matters are relative, after all, a question of perspective. Faithful. Unfaithful. Words like that cut two ways.

Dex liked the idea—words cutting two ways—liked it so much that he went to his overnight bag beside the bed. He unzipped it and dug down to find his journal. He opened the journal's nubby green cover to a fresh page and transcribed the idea in neat blue cursive, expanding on the thought—words cutting two ways.

The door lock clicked, and the door swung open. Dex slipped the book into his bag as the wide back end of a housekeeper appeared in the doorway, followed by a matching front end, a dragged vacuum cleaner, and a loosely grasped hank of electrical cord.

"Excuse me," Dex called to the housekeeper.

She gasped as she turned, her hand flying to her chest as if to catch an escaping heart. Her eyes, wide like a doll's, looked away, at the wall beside her, at the baseboard, at the floor.

"You'll have to come back." Belatedly, he flopped the blanket across his lap.

"*Perdóname, señor*," the woman said. Her fingers twisted a button on her salmon smock. "I see the lady leave. I think this room is empty."

"In a few minutes." He remembered now that LeAnn had made the reservation this time. "My wife." He felt his face flush at the lie. "She had an appointment."

The woman sniffed and looked toward the bathroom. "There is no smoking here," she said. "This is the rule."

Dex glanced at a bare wrist, his watch still on the nightstand. "Thirty minutes," he said.

"So sorry." The woman retreated, pulling her vacuum cleaner. "I will come back again when it is later. You will take all of your time, *señor*." The door clicked shut.

Dex shaved and showered, then turned on the television and clicked channels, settling finally on a European soccer match on ESPN. He glanced at this while he dressed. Then, from the bathroom, he retrieved his shaving gear, toothbrush, an unused soap and tiny shampoo. These he stuffed into his bag, padding them with clothes. Finally he took seven dollars from his wallet, folded the bills, and slid them into the housekeeper's tip envelope.

As he dropped the envelope on the desk, there was a timid tapping on the door. Dex checked his watch. Time to let housekeeping have their room back. "Come in." He flicked off the television and hoisted the sports-bag strap onto his shoulder.

The tapping came again, harder knuckles this time. "It's me," a voice whispered. "LeAnn."

He opened the door, and she slipped in. He caught her by the waist, pulled her close, and kissed her.

"No." She pushed away and fanned the air between them with her hands. "Perfume." As she said it, he smelled it, sweet as fruit gum. When he'd first warned LeAnn about Lovie's sensitive nose, she'd laughed. But she hadn't worn scent around him since. Not until now. She must have just put it on.

LeAnn edged past him and into the room. "My necklace, it's gone," she said, touching the hollow of her neck where it should hang. "I've looked everywhere."

"That Celtic thing?" Dex asked.

"It's a cross," she said, tilting an upholstered chair they'd shared, looking behind it. "A Celtic cross. You haven't seen it?" She flipped the bedclothes back, checked the folds, and then stripped the bed. She shook out the sheets, the blankets, the pillowcases.

He lifted the clock radio, the lamp, the Oberlin Inn memo pad and stubby pencil. From the bedside table, he pulled out the Gideon Bible and felt with his hand inside. Nothing. "You were wearing it last night."

"I know," she said, her eyes flaring at him. "Empty your bag."

"I just packed. It's not . . ." Desperation animated her face, moved every part of it in frantic ways. He unzipped the bag and spilled the contents onto the mattress pad, his journal buried in the pile. For a second he screened her vision. In that second he slid the journal under a pillow. Then, together, Dex and LeAnn pawed through his stuff.

LeAnn shook out his shirt, the one he'd worn yesterday, and the cross and chain flew out. They clanked against the base of the bedside lamp. Her hands clapped to her face, muffling a gasp. Dex retrieved the necklace from the floor. He restrung the cross, draped the chain around her neck. She held her hair aside, and Dex, behind her, fastened the clasp.

"I don't know what I'd do without it," she said. "It's been so lucky for me."

He held her shoulders, pulled her close, and kissed the nape of her neck where the clasp fell. As he did, he wondered what Lovie would have made of it, a Celtic cross necklace tangled in his dirty clothes? Would she wake up then? Would that famous nose finally smell the proverbial coffee? Or would she continue on,

chirpy and oblivious, content that Dex remained sober, uncon-
cerned with the spate of business trips now dotting his calendar?

"Easy, cowboy," LeAnn said. She turned to face him, a smile
lighting her eyes. "You'll need another shower."

"Check-out time isn't till eleven," Dex said.

Her hand landed weightlessly on his shoulder. She stretched up
and pecked a kiss on his cheek. "We have to go," she said. Then
she turned away, suddenly businesslike.

"Stay another day."

"I can't," she said, pulling herself free. "Lonnie will start
wondering."

2

Esperanza Tatengo turned the small book over in her hands, ran
her fingers across the gold-lettered, textured green cover as if
they might read what her eyes could not. The book looked like
something important, something official. Why then was it left
here beneath a bare pillow? The question puzzled her mind, and
she considered it for a long time. She should put it on her cleaning cart and turn it in to Mrs. Lutts, her supervisor. This was the
rule, and Esperanza had no desire for the attention that breaking
rules could bring. Still, the mysterious book enticed her.

She carefully opened the front cover, turned the first page, and
then another. The pages were ruled in columns like ones she had
seen at the immigration office, and she thought, yes, this book is
very important. But what she found inside did not look like official
records or numbers. Instead, English words looped and sprawled
across the pages, bright blue squiggles she could not read, some ar-
ranged in the form of poems with stanzas or verses. It occurred to
Esperanza that these might be prayer poems, the kind she herself
often composed for the Blessed Virgin Mary of Guadalupe. Such
writing she should expect. Was this not the uncommon man who
had removed from the drawer the Bible of Gideon to read? And had
he not left generous money in her tip envelope? True, some might
criticize that he smoked cigarettes against rules. Yet was it not also
true that many fine priests did do this, too?

Holding the book, she felt concern for what might become of these pages. Only last week her cousin, Maria Lucero, had turned in to Mrs. Lutts a sketchpad left behind by an artistic woman with much talent. Inside were sketched the bodies of people, their faces turned away. These bodies were strong, like the bodies of dancers, and their private parts were drawn with such bold detail as one might draw noses and ears. And later Mrs. Lutts showed these to many others only for their laughter. Esperanza felt great shame then, and even more the next day when she saw these sketches torn from the pad and hung from the dark walls of the utility room. Already they were defiled.

No, Esperanza thought, she must not allow such a fate for this man's poems. She slipped the book into the pocket of her smock. She would ask Maria's son Fabian, who worked nights in the lobby, to work the computer, to find the owner's name and address, and to print it on a card for her. In the morning she would mail this book to the man herself.

3

"That runt Eckert tells me I should leave more grinding stock," Lonnie McCray told his wife, LeAnn, as she came through the front door. He leaned against the casing of the kitchen doorway, his body a sharp angle, his hair still wet from the shower. A Budweiser bottle dangled from his two-fingered grip. "Can you believe that?"

LeAnn put the bright orange three-ring binder she'd been carrying on the end table and took her overnight bag to the bedroom. She felt relieved, seeing him now, still bound up in his small world. Still oblivious.

"Can you believe that?" he said again, as she came back up the hall. "Little prick not a year out of college, and he's telling me how to machine."

"What a jerk," LeAnn said on cue. She wondered if Lonnie had called his sister, Nan, if he'd offered to pick up their kids.

"'You do it my way,' Eckert tells me, 'or you clean out your locker.' I know he's bluffing. There's no way Nelson stands for it, that prick canning me."

She picked up the orange binder, held it for him to see. "I've got work to do at the table tonight. Insurance rate changes."

"I'm the best fucking machinist they've got," he said. "No one's close. Don't think they don't know."

"The place couldn't run without you," she said. It's something she'd heard him say a thousand times. Maybe it was true, maybe not. She parroted the line back to him anyway. That's what conversation with Lonnie had degenerated to—one man's opinions coming from two mouths. Her best friend, Tina, manager at Goddess Bods Exercise Emporium out at the mall, called it their "dynamic." LeAnn preferred to think of it as her contribution to family peace.

"Damned straight, it couldn't." Lonnie said. He looked at her oddly for an instant, really looked at her in a way that seemed disconnected from any thoughts of his boss or job. She wondered if he might have strayed for a moment from the center of his personal universe, and in straying he might have noticed that some things in this house didn't revolve around him. In fact, some things were slowly spinning away from him, if he'd bother opening his eyes to see. Whatever that odd look was, it vanished as quickly as it had arrived, replaced by the slightly frenzied look with which he usually related his day's struggles.

LeAnn would complain to Tina about how he'd changed, how he wasn't the man she'd fallen in love with, the man she'd married, the man who had taken her out of Spivey and Kentucky, brought her here to Dayton sixteen years ago. Even as she said it, though, she knew it wasn't completely true. Especially the part about him changing. In fact, Lonnie was the same, more or less. Maybe he'd put on a few pounds, and maybe he'd lost some of that boyish brashness, and maybe he took her for granted more than he did at first. That wasn't the heart of the problem, though. The heart of it was that, sometime around his twenty-seventh birthday, Lonnie McCray must have become precisely who he wanted to be. He stopped changing then, stopped changing completely. Sure, he still talked about a better job, talked about starting his own shop, talked about taking her on a real vacation—Hawaii, Cancun, some Caribbean island, maybe—but it was just talk. The last time anything changed with Lonnie must have been seven years ago. Maybe eight.

For her part, LeAnn was just beginning to change. As soon as daughter Bronwyn started preschool, LeAnn signed up for afternoon computer classes. Thinking back, she realized it was mostly about getting out of the house and being with grown-ups again. The whole computer aspect of it had been a lucky blunder, a quirk of class schedules. It could as easily have been beginning Spanish or calligraphy. She graduated into a job as billing assistant with a four-doctor clinic. Most of her early paychecks went for child care, but before that first year ended, the doctors had sent her to Indianapolis to learn insurance billing. Soon she was running the office. Now she had a checking account of her own, credit cards of her own, and interests of her own, not the least of which was relearning guitar. She'd always liked the way the instrument felt pressed against her, the way tones echoed out from the hollow body, the way strings would sometimes vibrate on their own, tingling her fingertips the instant she touched them. LeAnn bought a used electric guitar, a bright blue Fender with a cheap amp. She took lessons. She wanted to play slide, play it like Bonnie Raitt. She yearned to sing like her, too, although that was clearly impossible. "Can't," she explained to Tina. "I've got way too much Dolly Parton in my voice."

One day, halfway through their step aerobics set, Tina said in a matter-of-fact way, "You've grown apart." It summarized them neatly. Of course, Tina meant by that that it was mostly Lonnie who'd changed.

"Yes, we have," LeAnn said, resting for a moment on her step. "Most of that changing is mine." She felt a twinge of guilt. "Doesn't that violate a promise they hide in our wedding vows? A promise of constancy, of forever, of always being there?" LeAnn fell into step with Tina and the music again. Okay, she was the one who'd changed, who was still changing, in fact. Still, she wanted Tina to see it the other way, to believe that Lonnie had changed, that he was the one to blame.

To tell the truth, there had been one change in her husband. In their early years together, he'd always held his temper with her. Always. She'd acted so meek around him, it was no wonder. At times she'd seen him explode at his brother, his hands clenched into fists, his face tight and thrust forward, his voice rasped, his neck corded and red. She'd seen him blow up at their boys, Adam and Scott, lose it over wet bedclothes or broken toys. He'd never lost his temper with their daughter though.

Or, until recently, with LeAnn.

She couldn't pinpoint exactly when things changed, when she'd become worthy of his wrath. Two years ago, maybe three. It had been a gradual thing. He hadn't hit her. No, he'd never done that. But all the words were there, the anger, the obscene shouts, the fists drawn up and ready to strike. Her heart told her it was only a matter of time.

She'd trained herself to retreat to a benign, nodding place, a place of nondisagreement, whenever Lonnie started to steam. It was like summoning a rubber version of herself, one who'd sit and nod, his angry words bouncing off without harm while the real LeAnn hovered in a high corner of the room, safe and unseen. In fact, this pseudoself had become such a good listener and reflex responder that she'd often call on her when Lonnie droned on about his work, his boss, how they couldn't get along without him.

Like now.

She called after him as he headed down the hall toward the bathroom, "Did you call Nan? About the kids?"

"What time did you tell her you'd be back?" he asked through the open door.

"Today is all I said."

"Let her keep them for supper," he said. "They're good company for her three. You heard her say so."

"I really should call," LeAnn said. "Let her know."

"Hey," he called over the sound of flushing water, "we've got the house to ourselves. What's your rush?"

"I miss them," she answered. It was true, in a way. "I'm beat," she added quickly. This was also true and more to his point about the house without kids. "It's been a long day, a long drive. I should unpack, fix something for supper."

"I could pick up a pizza," Lonnie said, coming back up the hall. "And the kids?"

"Didn't I just say Nan can keep them a little longer?"

"At least we should let her know—"

"Jesus, babe. We've got the whole goddamn house to ourselves. Let's enjoy it! I'll open a couple beers. I'll put music on, whatever you like." He opened the refrigerator. "What'll you have? Bud? Coors? Heineken?"

"Whatever you're having," she called out. "Okay with you if I put on Enya?"

"Whatever turns you on," Lonnie said.

That'd be Dex, a quiet voice inside answered. A wave of sweet warmth washed over LeAnn. She went to the CD player, loaded the carousel with three disks, all Enya, and pushed play. According to Tina, no one could possibly like both Bonnie Raitt and Enya, not at the same time. Musically impossible, she said. LeAnn knew better. Bonnie fed her spirit, Enya her soul. All a matter of mood, she'd told Tina. Mood and appetite.

Lonnie handed her a Budweiser, the bottle cold and slick in her hand. She took a sip, just enough to wet her mouth, and held it on her tongue for a few seconds before swallowing. That first taste was always the best.

"If you had your own Bridgeport," she said, letting her voice trail off.

"I know I keep saying it, not doing it," he said. "Days like today, I know that's what I'm meant to do—have my own place, my own machines. All it'd take is a small Bridgeport. You can pick one up in decent shape for six grand. Eight tops. Put another five into the gibs and ways, get her good and tight, and you've got a machine that'll run another fifty years."

She moved a stack of the boys' game cartridges from the couch to the coffee table, picked up Bronwyn's bright yellow sweater, buttoned and folded it, and placed it on the table, too. Then she settled beside Lonnie on the couch, flipped off her shoes, and curled her legs beneath her. Mystic chant music flowed through the room. It soothed a small fluttering under her ribs.

"Wouldn't have to be digital, as long as it's tight," he said. "Lonnie McCray doesn't need NC to handle a Bridgeport, not like those tech-school kids." Sometimes he talked like that about himself, like he was some other person, someone famous.

Enya's voice and plucked harp strings told LeAnn to sail away, and she did. She sailed on wings of Celtic harmony, on one crystalline voice above a chanting chorus, a primitive flute, drumbeats knocking at doors deep inside her. She couldn't make out the words, English-sounding but not English. They seemed so mystic, so sacred, so wise, this woman sweet-talking her soul. LeAnn's hand went to the Celtic cross at the hollow of her neck. Was it just this morning that Dex had fastened it there? She remembered his lips, how they'd felt on her neck, his hands on her shoulders pulling her to him. A shiver raced up her spine.

Lonnie laughed. "Someone walk across your grave?"

Yours, she thought. "I guess," she said, looking away.

He downed the rest of his beer, and LeAnn handed him hers. It was still nearly full. "Anyways," he continued, "the garage is the obvious place. She'll need a footing, one at least two-foot deep, say five by eight. I'd pour it myself, save a couple hundred right there. Stable platform's important for a machine like that. And heat, we'll need heat out there, too, in the garage. Good heat, heat on a thermostat."

He'd worked all this out for the bank, planned it with his brother, Jack, two years ago, when he'd first applied for the loan. Jack helped draw up a business plan for Lonnie McCray and Sons, Custom Tool and Die. They'd figured it all, what he'd need, what it'd cost, how he'd pay the bank back in three years. According to Lonnie, the problem was that bankers have no vision. They play safe. He counted on a few of Nelson's customers going with him. Just a few, that's all it'd take. Everyone knew he could do the work.

"Damn banker. He expected commitments, signed contracts, for Christ sake," he'd told her when he got home that day.

She still wondered if the bank might have come up with some kind of loan. Maybe they'd have considered a second mortgage on the house. But Lonnie had gotten steamed at the loan officer's questions. He gave the young man his candid opinion of bankers, told him what he could do with his precious money, and stormed out. Over the next few months, this evolved into a story that Lonnie loved telling, one he shaped into a sidesplitting tale of a room full of bankers, dumbfounded, jaws locked open, as Lonnie, in this re-telling, enlightens them on their shortsighted ways.

LeAnn padded barefoot into the kitchen and returned with two more beers. She handed one to Lonnie and sipped the other.

"Thanks, babe," he said. "Piecing away at it, that's the key. Footings aren't that difficult. Concrete. Has to be massive, though. Two feet thick, minimum."

He'd started piecing away last year, wood-burning a six-foot-long pine sign—McCray & Sons, Custom Tool & Die. It hung in the garage, facing the wall so no one would see, so no one would tell Nelson that his ace machinist might be going out on his own.

LeAnn curled against him, her head on his shoulder, her hand on his chest. His arm went around her, and she shifted closer. She liked the familiar smell of him, slightly musky, with a hint of machine oil that lingered even after he'd showered. It was the smell of his work, the smell of lathes and grinders and milling machines. And it was not so different, LeAnn remembered, from the smell of her father, the smell of locomotives.

"Someone mentioned pizza?" she said.

His arm loosened, his hand slipped off her hip. He checked his wristwatch. "Shit," he said. "You hungry?"

Hell yes, she was hungry. "A little," she said.

"There one in the freezer?"

"We ate it." There might be another pizza, the cardboard kind, buried somewhere in back, but that wasn't what she wanted. "Give me your keys," she said, reaching for her shoes. "I'll go." She'd pick up their kids from Nan, too.

"Hello," Lonnie said. "They deliver." He said it in a singsong way, meaning how stupid could she be.

She sat back, a shoe in her hand.

"Jeez, LeAnn," he said, draping an arm around her again. "Can't we just sit here and relax for a few minutes?"

She turned to look at him, ran her fingers through the thick, dark hair on the side of his head, fingered it over and behind his ear. "Okay," she said softly. "Just let me phone the order in first." She bounced to her feet. "Pepperoni?"

"Get extra cheese, too," he said. "They been stingy with the cheese lately, cutting corners, like maybe we won't notice."

The boy on the phone said they had orders backed up, it would be thirty-five minutes, maybe longer. LeAnn ordered anyway, a large double-cheese and pepperoni for them and a medium sausage with olives, something to reheat if the kids came home hungry. With Lonnie's sister, Nan, you never quite knew.

"Fifteen minutes?" Lonnie asked as she settled back beside him.

"Something like that," she answered. He frowned and turned

on the TV, the Weather Channel. Together, they waited for pizza and the weekly weather planner.

A half hour later, LeAnn heard car brakes outside. "I'll get it," she said. She grabbed her wallet from the table by the door.

"Ridiculous!" Lonnie leaned forward and checked his watch. "Thirty-two minutes. It's probably cold by now. Nothing's worse than cold pepperoni."

Off the top of her head, she could name a few thousand things worse than cold pepperoni. Lonnie himself was climbing that list. "Hush," she said, and she opened the door.

"Don't you dare tip the kid, not one goddamn dime!" He shouted it loud enough for the delivery boy to hear—if there had been a delivery boy at the door, which there was not. Instead, Adam and Scott bounded onto the porch and through the doorway. Walking up the sidewalk behind them was Nan. The normally prim woman's hair looked slightly spiky. Her thin lips were outlined bright red, but they weren't filled in, giving her weary face the look of an unfinished page in a child's coloring book. She carried Bronwyn, carried the chubby-legged girl on her hip like a whiny two-year-old.

"Is she all right?" LeAnn asked.

"She threw up at the supper table," Nan said, climbing the stairs. "I doubt it's anything serious, though. The boys were teasing her, telling her tofu burgers are made from frog guts."

"They're not really," Bronwyn said. "Boys just like to be gross. Right, Aunt Nan?" The girl squirmed to get down, her whininess suddenly gone.

"I am so sorry," LeAnn said. "Thanks for watching—"

"Hope they weren't a bother, sis," Lonnie said, joining LeAnn in the doorway.

"They're boys," Nan said, a failed attempt at a smile creasing her face.

"LeAnn just got in. Long drive, Kentucky," Lonnie said. "We were about to come over, pick them up, take them off your hands."

"Saved you a trip." Nan's eyes looked tired as a hound's.

"Thanks again," LeAnn said as Nan turned to leave. "Really. I owe you."

"Wait, sis," Lonnie called after her. "Have a beer before you go."

At the bottom of the stairs, Nan turned and looked up. "I don't drink anything alcoholic, Lonnie. I haven't for nearly five years now."

"There's your problem." Lonnie said it loud enough for LeAnn to hear over the boys' commotion behind her, but not loud enough for his sister to catch.

A tiny muscle in LeAnn's cheek twitched, winking her eye. She wanted a cigarette, wanted one now. She wished she hadn't foolishly tossed out the pack as she crossed the Ohio River, the pack Dex had bought her at the motel. She wished she could step onto the porch, close the door behind her, and light one now. Just a few puffs, that's all she'd need right now.

As Nan walked back to her car, the pizza delivery van pulled into the driveway, blocking her. Alone in the doorway, LeAnn watched her get into the car and start the engine. Nan waited there, revving the engine, while the delivery boy hurried up the walk.

LeAnn took the pizzas. Balancing the hot boxes on her bare forearm, she fumbled in her wallet, managing finally to pull out a twenty-dollar bill and a five. "Keep the change," she said, and she carried the boxes to the kitchen table.

Someone—Scott, she guessed—had switched music on the CD player, switched to something that seemed barely music. "You know the rules," she said. "Your music stays in your room. It gives me a headache."

"Yours makes me puke," Scott muttered. An angry sort of sullenness was taking root in her oldest son. She saw it now in the way he shuffled across to the player, in the way he poked the power button with a defiant middle finger.

This is where Lonnie, who'd grabbed a slice of pizza without waiting for plates, should've said something, should've said anything to back her up. He didn't, though. He never did. Other times, she'd asked him why. He'd said that one parent should be able to handle a kid, that two-on-one amounted to ganging up. And that, he'd said, wasn't fair to the kid. Boys needed room to breathe and grow. Maybe he was right. Still, Scott was getting to the point where a little ganging up might be in order. And Adam, could he be far behind?

LeAnn set plastic plates and forks on the table and poured three glasses of Coke.

"Aunt Nan says that Cokes are poison," Bronwyn said, pushing her glass away.

"She's so weird," Adam said. He meant Nan.

"Eat, son," Lonnie said. "Stop running your mouth." He glared at Adam until the boy grabbed a slice and started eating. Then he turned to Bronwyn. "Listen to me, young lady. Coke is good for you." He looked across to LeAnn then, and he winked. "See," his wink seemed to say, "I do help with the kids."

LeAnn had lost what little appetite she'd had. She idly wound strings of cheese around the tines of her fork and scraped them clean between her teeth. Across the table, Lonnie ate fast, big bites, like a dog. Soon the children had finished off their pizza and started on the larger one. With careful fingers, Bronwyn picked pepperoni from her slice, dropping the red circles onto a paper towel. "It's all slimy," she said, wiping her fingers on her shirt-front after each piece.

Lonnie picked up one of her discarded pepperoni between finger and thumb, raised it over his gaping mouth, and dropped it in. "I love slimy." He swallowed and laughed diabolically, made crazy eyes, licked his fingers with loud, kissing noises. The boys joined in, mimicking him, laughing, snatching the pieces away, battling each other for the meat circles. When the last was eaten, the boys stripped pepperoni from the three slices left in the box.

Later, as LeAnn rinsed out the glasses at the sink, she wished she'd put out real plates, real knives and forks. She'd wash them now, wash them by hand in a sink filled with sudsy water. She'd take off her wristwatch and rings, put them up on the windowsill, and she'd bury her hands and arms to the elbows in suds. She'd scrub those dishes clean, rinse them in a cold spray, stand them to drain on the other side. She'd dig in a drawer to find an old dish-towel, one worn thin with a faded calendar, and she'd wipe every-thing dry, clean glasses sparkling, clean dishes squeaky beneath her thumb.

As she rinsed the glasses, she gazed out the window into the backyard. Evening light had dimmed. The fence shadow fell across a weedy patch. For years it had been her vegetable garden, but now the patch was overgrown, dense with leafy ragweed and rust-colored curly dock stalks, the pods heavy and bursting with seeds. High in the lone white oak tree, the ends of two frayed ropes swayed in the evening breeze, flicking at slant sunrays that still filtered through the branches. Years ago, her father and Lonnie had strung ropes over a thick limb, and they'd hung a swing from the tree, a porch swing for which LeAnn and Lonnie had no porch.

Bronwyn went to her bedroom to watch *The Little Mermaid*. The boys plopped down on the floor, backs against the couch, matching control boxes cradled on their laps, and they played Dynamo Crash X-Quest on the big TV screen.

"News flash," Lonnie said. "Bengals play the Browns tonight. Thursday Night Football. Eight o'clock."

"So?" Adam said.

Lonnie gave his younger son a glancing slap on the back of his head, a not-so-playful one. "So-o," he said, stretching the word, "so your game ends at eight, no matter what." Then his voice grew serious, his words clipped. "And don't you start with the smart mouth like your brother."

Scott turned and looked at his father, glared at him for a moment before he returned his attention to the game. LeAnn, watching from the kitchen doorway, hugged her arms across her stomach and tried not to think of the years ahead, the boys growing into their teens.

At eight o'clock the boys unhooked the game and took it to the small TV in their bedroom. "You can't hardly see the kill counts," Scott muttered, dragging control cords behind him.

"You got it so bad," Lonnie said. His voice sounded hard. He came to his feet, started to follow Scott to his room. LeAnn caught her husband's arm at the head of the hallway, stopped him before he went further, before he said what he intended. She saw the frustration on his face. She knew it well. It hummed inside her, too, reverberated, a tight vibration like an unplucked string.

"Not tonight, Lonnie," she said. "Let it go."

And so Lonnie watched his ballgame, the boys battled by proxy on a too-small screen, Scott smoking Adam, he trumpeted. LeAnn spread her notebook at the kitchen table to work. And Bronwyn fell asleep in a pile of plush toys sometime before mermaid Ariel traded her voice to the evil Ursula. LeAnn pulled the plug on the boys at nine thirty, sending them groaning to their bunks. In the dark they waged verbal skirmishes for another hour before sleep finally called a temporary truce.

By the end of the third quarter, with the Bengals down by three touchdowns and a field goal, Lonnie gave up. He flicked off the TV, vowing he'd never watch another game. From the refrigerator he grabbed a slice of stripped pizza. He paced the kitchen while he ate, chewing loudly, peering over LeAnn's shoulder as she filed away the revised insurance codes. He ate all but the rim crust, which he offered to LeAnn. When she declined with a wave of her hand, he shoved the crust down the garbage disposal, chasing it away with water.

He stooped and kissed her cheek, his breath alive with the tang of oregano and tomato sauce. She did not look up. "Night, babe," he said, and he started down the hall.

"Be there in a minute," she promised. Beneath the chair, her ankles were crossed, so it wouldn't count as a lie.

By midnight, her mind a sieve, LeAnn closed the binder. She pulled on a jacket, slipped out the back door, and sat on the second step. The night air was quiet, chilly and clear. The white oak loomed, still as a photograph, dark against a starry night sky. She ran a hand along the wood step. She liked how it felt, rounded along the edge, smoothed and slightly cupped by the traffic of shoes. The chill air tingled her cheeks, her neck, the backs of her hands. She combed her fingers through her hair, spreading it, letting it slowly come free of her fingers and fall. Somewhere blocks away, a dog barked, not an angry bark but the slow, lonely kind. LeAnn leaned back on her elbows, looked up, and tried to pick out the one star that was directly overhead. She couldn't tell, though, couldn't decide. The heavens seemed to quiver, to swim in the heat of her rising breath.

They were all sleeping now. She had this time, and she wanted to think things out, understand where she stood, about Dex, about Lonnie. She needed to make sense of it, how she'd ended up in this tangled life, a haphazard life, a life that seemed somehow not truly hers at all. If she could only make sense of it, what she wanted, what she needed, maybe then she'd know what to do. Maybe she'd find a way then to stop careening, to gain some direction and control. But leaning back, all she saw were dark branches, motionless against a shimmering, star-flecked sky.

It was late. The Quick Mart three blocks away would be open, though. She'd walk there, walk slowly. Maybe a bit of muscle and bone motion, flesh moving in fabric, would help her think, would stir the air, maybe shake her fate loose from this reluctant world.

Besides, she really needed a cigarette.

4

Lonnie McCray wasn't buying the forecast. The so-called experts on the Weather Channel had predicted a sunny Saturday. Unseasonably warm for late October, they said. Lonnie knew better. Their forecasts usually turned out to be flat wrong. He could do better flipping a coin.

Even though it was Saturday, LeAnn had rolled out of bed early and dressed for work. His wife was behind with billings at the clinic. Or so she said. Lonnie wondered, though. Hell, anyone in his right mind would wonder, the way she'd been acting lately.

It wasn't so much the way her mind seemed to wander when he talked to her, although that was part of it. No, it was more about her screwed-up way of seeing things. It started with Tina, the ball buster LeAnn exercised with at the mall, the one whose words she quoted as though this woman knew just everything about everything. There was something suspicious there. And that weird Celtic crap, the music and jewelry and scarves—where did that come from? And where was it all leading LeAnn? He'd been so wrapped up in his business plans, so preoccupied, that he'd let this shit go too far. That went for the kids, too. LeAnn was spoiling them. And he was letting her.

Lonnie considered himself a patient man. But with the boys, he'd been patient too long. He should have stepped in earlier and laid down a law or two. He was their father, after all, the man of this house. In a way, he'd let them down. From now on, though, he'd do better. He'd give them chores around the place, like he'd had growing up. He'd make them toe the line. He'd teach them what it meant to be part of this family. And he'd make sure LeAnn got strict with them, too.

At ten o'clock, he phoned the office just to be sure LeAnn was there, reminding her when she answered that he was out of Swiss cheese. She promised to be home by two o'clock. He intended to hold her to it.

After hanging up the phone, Lonnie pulled the plugs on the TV and video games, and he shooed the kids outside. He'd start them with a simple chore—raking leaves from the front and back lawns into piles and bagging them. In the garage he found a toy plastic rake for Bronwyn and full-sized rakes for the boys. Scott got the fanned bamboo one, Adam the one with springy green metal prongs. They stomped and groaned, but before long, warm morning sunshine and crisp, ankle-deep leaves changed their moods. Soon they were raking up waist-deep piles and romping through them.

As he opened the garage door, a hint of burnt-pine smell greeted him, a faint reminder of the acrid smell as he'd burned letters into his McCray & Sons sign. He touched the back of the sign, the rough, splintery wood he intended to stain. He'd do it soon, maybe tomorrow.

Lonnie backed his car, an eight-year-old Chevy, down the driveway and onto the street. He parked it there with the passenger-side wheels riding up the curb and onto the yard. The car wasn't due for an oil change for another eight hundred miles, but he couldn't count on better weather until spring. With a flat metal pan in one hand and a wrench and rag in the other, Lonnie lay back in the leaf-filled gutter and slid himself under the car. The grimy underside of the car skimmed past his nose, its scent like new asphalt and grease. He eased himself back past the radiator and front axle to the oil drain plug, sliding to one side with a leafy rustle to clamp his wrench on the plug. He loosened it until oil started to seep out. Then he slid the pan under and unscrewed the plug by hand. It came free and dropped from his fingers into the pan in a gush of slick black. Lonnie wiped his fingers with the rag, and, pressing his heels against the pavement, skidded his way back into blinding sunlight. He stood and he stretched, feeling warm and righteous in the late October warmth. Okay, this once the Weather Channel got it right.

Lonnie unlatched the Chevy's hood and lifted it. He bent into the engine compartment, and, as he slipped the band of his spanner wrench over the oil filter, he heard a sharp beep. He let go of the spanner and straightened up. The mailman, a slight man with sunken cheeks, a ruddy complexion, and dark caterpillar eyebrows that seemed to kiss where they met, sat in his open cart in the middle of the street. He had mail clutched in his extended hand. "Can't reach your mailbox," he said. "Car's in the way." A perplexed look wrinkled his face, as though this presented an unsolvable problem.

All he'd have to do was step out and walk over—six steps. Either that option eluded the man, or it violated some postal regulation. Whatever the case, the helpless man sat with the mail sticking out until Lonnie threw his rag on the lawn and walked around to take it from him. Something like a smile formed on the mailman's face, his mouth square and toothy, his eyes uninvolved. "Thank you," he said. His voice was flat and vaguely mocking. The vehicle's tiny engine revved, its sound like a toy, as it drove away.

"Fuck you, too," Lonnie muttered. "Fuck you very much."

As Lonnie walked up the driveway, he flipped through the stack. All junk mail and bills until, at the bottom, he came to a thick bubble envelope. It was addressed in an awkward, childish hand to LeAnn, the return address in Somerset, Kentucky.

He didn't know anyone in Somerset. There was no return address, no name there. He turned the envelope over in his hands, shook it, and then squeezed it so hard that bubbles popped under his thumbs. It felt like a plaque or a book or maybe a videotape, although it didn't seem thick enough for that. Inside the front door, he dropped the mail on the hall table and went to the kitchen to wash the grime from his hands. As he lathered and rinsed, Lonnie couldn't get the package out of his mind. He dried his hands on paper towels, grabbed a steak knife from the silverware drawer, and went back to the hall table. Pushing the other mail aside, he picked up the package, and he slit it open.

A green book slid out. Lonnie felt a small rush of satisfaction at having guessed right. Taped to the textured cover was a small yellow note:

This book was leaved in room 176 and is
returned now for you.
May God bless you always.

There was no signature.

It's a mistake, Lonnie thought, a screw-up of some sort. He opened the book. Maybe he'd find a name inside, some clue to the owner. He flipped back to the first page, but there was no name there, only writing—entries, like a diary. The handwriting was much larger and loopier than LeAnn's.

Thumbing through, he saw the name Dexter Chalk, and for a few seconds it meant nothing to Lonnie, not until he had turned another two pages. Then it hit like a thousand-volt jolt, dropping him into a chair.

Dex Chalk.

Dexter Chalk. He'd been LeAnn's boyfriend in high school, the one still living back in Spivey. Lonnie stood again. He paced the hall and read, bumped into a table, a chair, his mind trapped in the pages. There were affirmations to get Dex through the day. There were meditations on someone named Lovie, on the hundred ways she'd let him down. And there was a poem to LeAnn, the joy she'd brought to his life, their shared rediscovery of life's sweet ecstasy. The words went jittery. His eyes skipped across them, skipped ahead, skipped away from the page like the wrong magnet pole. They refused to read more than a phrase here and there. They tried to protect him, tried to limit the pain.

"Daddy." Bronwyn slapped at the screen door two-handed. "Daddy!"

"Go play," Lonnie shouted.

"But Daddy—"

"Don't you listen?" he yelled and started toward her.

The girl stumbled back. "They lit matches," she cried, "and now they can't get the fires stamped out."

Lonnie raced outside. Adam and Scott stomped frantically at the edge of the largest blaze. Burning leaves flew up around their pant legs. Flaring embers drifted up and away to light new fires. "Get away!" Lonnie yelled. "You're making it worse." He ran to the other side of the house, unhooked the hose, and dragged the coil around to the front. He screwed it onto the faucet behind the juniper bushes, turned on the water, and aimed the spray at the fires.

"Let me," Scott said, a kind of thrill in his voice. The boy grabbed for the hose, tried to pull it from Lonnie's grasp.

Lonnie yanked it away, and his hand swung toward the boy, the back of it hitting him flush between his ear and eye. It didn't seem such a hard blow to Lonnie, but the boy fell to his knees and toppled over. He stayed there for the longest time, even after the last flames were out, and the soaked black leaf piles were left to smolder.

Lonnie sent Adam and Bronwyn to their rooms. He wrapped ice cubes in a towel for Scott to help with the bruise swelling under his eye. Then he sent the boy to the garage. There would be no lunch, not for any of them. Not for Lonnie, either.

It was nearly two o'clock when Lonnie raked together the last of the charred leaves, the scraps and crumbs of other piles, gathering the dregs to bag. The smell of damp char still hung in the air. His hands were black, his shoes soot-smudged. Tears pooled in his eyes, and a lump of something like grief weighed him down. Lonnie didn't know what he'd do, how he'd look at LeAnn, how he'd hold what he knew inside and not explode. How did she do it, he wondered. How did she live here with him and screw another man? How could she without dissolving?

He'd forgotten to put on gloves. Blisters the size of quarters lay flat and wet on his palms. He didn't care. The work felt good to Lonnie. The pull on his shoulders was an ache now, a good kind of ache. This was an honest feeling, the rake tines tugging through the grass, his sweat-soaked shirt clinging to his back, this sweet stinging on his hands.

The rhythm of the work had helped him think. He'd been too distracted. That was it. He'd been too easy, too lax. He hadn't paid attention, hadn't thought things through. He needed to be patient now, to not rush, to find a way to get things back like they were. He'd cage his anger, not act rashly this time. He'd take his time, handle things carefully, do what he must to mend his family. And if that wasn't possible? No, he couldn't think about that, not now. If he did, he'd be lost.

LeAnn came home at two seventeen, as Lonnie stacked the last two leaf bags at the curb. He didn't mention the time. At the door, he slipped off his shoes and followed her into the kitchen. Without once looking at his wife, he told her about the fire, the kids in their rooms, Scott's eye. Then Lonnie showered. He lathered again and again, trying to wash the horrid ash smell from his skin and hair, to get it out of his pores.

That evening, as Lonnie watched three slick college kids play Jeopardy on TV, LeAnn, looking out the front window, asked if he was leaving the car on the street overnight. He remembered the oil drained in the pan then, the hood raised, the spanner wrench still on the filter.

"It'll be there in the morning," Lonnie said without looking up from the screen.

LeAnn came over to him and nudged against his knee. "Mind if I join you?" Lonnie shifted to make room, and she settled beside him. Her head lolled onto his shoulder. Her hand lay lightly on his chest, rising and falling with his breath.

A faint aroma of tobacco smoke came up to Lonnie McCray from his wife's hair. Her smoke smell seemed such an odd thing to him, so flat, so different from the hint of leaf-char smell still on him. And neither was like the faintly acrid aroma that Lonnie could swear he smelled just then, the wood-burned scent of the pine sign hanging in the garage.

Marathon Man

Jack loosens his bow tie, slides the suspenders from his shoulders, and, holding his breath, waits for the sounds. They will come from behind him, from the dressing table across the room. He hears a swish as Dianne steps from her emerald satin dress, preparing the air, or so he imagines, for the tiny sounds that will follow.

He has heard them perhaps a dozen times before. But he has dreamed them hundreds more—studded pearls dropped on glass, their plink so distinct the sounds are etched on his brain.

For reasons of sanitation, Dianne does not keep her dressy earrings, the expensive pearls with surgical steel posts, in the felt-lined, walnut box Jack gave her on their tenth anniversary. Instead, she keeps them in a covered petrie dish that she hides above her bathroom medicine cabinet. She wears the pearls only on special occasions—christenings, church weddings, close family funerals, and their landmark wedding anniversaries, those divisible by five.

Neither does she keep her everyday earrings in the felt-lined box. They have their own dish.

Dianne worries about germs. When she was a teenager, the hole in her left earlobe developed an angry red infection. Only after a doctor cauterized the wound did the infection finally clear. Thirty years later, she recounts that episode frequently, usually at bedtime, seated, as she is now, before her mirror. She fingers the gray-smudge spot, inspecting the blemish that never quite disappeared.

Jack hears the clasp of his wife's pearl necklace—the good pearls, the ones never lent—as it snakes across the table and into the box. Then the pearls coil in with a tiny tic-tic-tic, joining other jewelry in the box. Most is expensive, and all is well chosen, built to clip, or hook, or snap and dangle, or slip onto fingers or wrists.

But nothing having posts touches felt. Nothing that penetrates.

Plink. The first earring lands on glass. Then a faint swish as it rolls about in the dish, settling, like a bowling pin rolling on hardwood.

Dianne says, "They should be happy."

"It's a crapshoot," he says, quickly adding, "you're right, they should."

"She'll be with family." As she says this, the second pearl plinks into the dish, ricocheting billiardlike against the first. Both roll and settle, barely audible in the shallow glass dish. "His family, of course," she says, "but family, nonetheless."

"Toronto's not so far." Jack turns at last to face his wife's reflection in the mirror. "She'll come visit."

"Will she?" She fingers aside a strand of platinum hair that wanders her forehead.

"Of course she will." He feels his words stumble on doubt.

Turning from her mirror, she extends a hand. "You are a dear." Jack takes it, raises it up, and kisses the palm. It feels slick with the coconut-scented cream she applies around her eyes. When he releases the hand, she slides the back of it along his jaw, touching his cheek and chin. If this were Friday, her caress would be an invitation.

But this is Saturday.

Last night, Friday night, when he kissed her bare shoulder, she begged off. "Big day ahead. Losing a daughter," she said. "Not gaining a son."

And the wedding has drained them both.

She pours rubbing alcohol over her earrings, drenching them, sanitizing them. The sharp smell tweaks his nostrils, reminding him of flu shots, of cold gauze swabbed high on his arm, of the deep muscle stabs that followed.

He retreats to the kitchen and mixes a screwdriver that is more vodka than orange juice. She was talking when the second earring hit glass. He hadn't counted on that, had never imagined the moment that way, all those times imagining it.

Still, facts are facts.

He has heard the pearls drop for the last time.

He's endured through it all. He's stayed the course, and nothing holds him now. His drink goes down sweet. The vodka slides warm inside him, warm like good love.

Alone in a dark kitchen, Jack remembers Boston, remembers meeting a young woman there centuries ago.

An applauding crowd lined Pru Plaza. "Incredible!" the young woman said. Somehow she managed to blend a groan with a laugh. She wrapped her sweaty arms around Jack's equally sweaty neck and, for a moment, rested her forehead against his chest. "My first time under three hours," she said between labored breaths.

"Mine, too." Jack checked his watch again to be sure. "2:59:10."

"You pulled me those last three miles," she said. "Did you know?"

Someone handed them orange sections. She sucked on hers and laughed again as pulpy juice dribbled down her chin and onto her lime green singlet.

He had seen her first climbing Newton Hills, noticed her running ahead of him, running strong among men, elbows swinging wide, knees still pumping two-thirds of the way to the crest. Hers was a runner's build, slender, long-legged. Passing her, he glanced sideways, even as he struggled for air, looking for breasts and trying, for at least those few strides beside her, to not gasp too desperately.

Someone draped reflective foil blankets over them and led them between ropes to a tented lawn swarming with bright-clad runners. Passing a table, he grabbed two bottles of water and handed one to her. "You local?"

"Hardly," she said. She shrugged off her blanket and, bending forward, poured water behind her neck. "Place called Erlanger, outside Cincinnati."

"Big Red Machine." Jack said, immediately feeling stupid for saying something so trite.

"You?"

"Spivey. Place you never heard of two hours to your south."

Her eyes brightened. "I know it," she said, sounding amazed. She crossed her ankles then, and, bending straight-legged, grasped the backs of her calves. Her nose touched a knee. "You at the Copley?"

"Down the street. The Westin."

"Copley has this fantastic buffet set up for runners." She straightened and stretched her arms high, leaning first left and then right. "Great bar, too."

"Maybe I'll stop by." Jack knew full well he would.

"Do that," she said. "We can rehydrate together." She reached a hand under his shirt and spider-walked it around his side, her fingernails electric on his skin. "Maybe check each other's pulse rate," she said.

He bumped his hip against hers. "Stamina, flexibility, that sort of thing?"

A crooked smile played on her face. "I'll be at the bar. Five o'clock."

An hour later, Jack realized he didn't know the woman's name. Nor could he recall anything remarkable about her face, except a sometimes crooked smile. What he did remember was her runner's number, her finishing time, and her juice-splattered lime green singlet, none of which would help locate her in a crowded bar.

Except one detail had snagged his eye as she stretched before him like an angular ballerina—a dark patch, small, like a pencil stab through her left earlobe. If she didn't cover it with earrings, he'd recognize her by that.

Back in the bedroom, Jack undresses and slips between sheets. Dianne sleeps, or if she does not sleep, her slow, rhythmic breathing says she wishes to be treated as sleeping. A taunting aroma of rubbing alcohol lingers in the room.

Sometimes he talks with her in his head, stages safe arguments, supplying her lines as well as his. He knows her that well.

"Do you know," he asks her in his mind, "or even suspect that a young you, fresh and alive, visits this bed?" It was true. The eager athlete of Copley, the carnal woman of their youthful couplings, his sensual bride, they sometimes visited his dreams, tempting him away from this other woman, the one they will become.

"Grow up, Jack," she would say. "There's more than that to life."

"There's less, too." He feels a sinking inside, as if in an elevator starting down.

"I always suspected without that . . ." She would use her annoying, knowing tone.

He interrupts. "It's more. Don't reduce it to that."

"Then what? Is this a midlife thing? Your male menopause?" She'd do that, try to name it, label it, pigeonhole it so she won't have to deal.

"Don't you remember? Us together?"

"Face facts. Our libidos aren't twenty-one anymore."

"You're not listening. It's more than that."

But she'd go back to it again, hearing only herself, not him. "I'd be nothing to you without that."

He rises to the imagined bait. "So you withhold, you ration . . ."

He's certain that she'd cut him off there. "Don't you dare say that."

So he doesn't say it all, not even in imaginary dialogues. He could shake her from sleep, or fake sleep, and ask these things outright. But it does no good, serves no purpose, turning their old ground.

Sleep sends its fog.

It's all too dispersed.

Her pearls disinfect in the bathroom.

Their baby's gone to Toronto, maybe forever.

His worn Sauconys hang in the basement, lace-tied, slung over a pipe.

The hills of Newton lie 920 miles to the east.

And the young woman with no name, the woman who laughs through dripped juice, is nowhere to be found.

Prologue

(two lives in letters)

October 7, 1963

Mr. Davis Menifee, Jr.
P.O. Box 47
Colton Creek Road
Spivey, Kentucky

Dear Mr. Menifee:
On behalf of the entire Kentucky congressional delegation, the Hon. John Sherman Cooper, United States Senator, is pleased to inform you of your selection as an alternate delegate representing this Commonwealth at the 1963 Congressional Youth Leadership Conference to be held November 23 through November 30 in Washington, D.C.

America's bright future depends on our producing young leaders at all levels of society. Your record of civic involvement and scholastic excellence at Burkitt County High School gives strong evidence of your potential. The goal of the Youth Leadership Conference is to help you develop that potential and become a leader of your generation, the generation that will eventually be handed the reins of leadership in our country's pursuit of domestic prosperity and the defense of freedom in this troubled world. Along with other outstanding youth from across this great land, you will be encouraged to participate in discussing the critical issues, both foreign and domestic, facing us today and into the future. We anticipate that senior representatives of the executive, legislative, and judicial branches will join the discussions as their time allows.

All primary and alternate delegates will receive information on bus schedules and housing arrangements from this office within two weeks. We have not been advised of specific assignments for this year's conference. Last year the Kentucky boys' delegation stayed at Georgetown University, and our two young lady representatives were housed with their counterparts from other states at American University.

If you have been selected as a primary delegate and you are unable to attend, please advise this office at the earliest practical date. Alternates will be notified if openings occur.

Congratulations on your selection. The entire Kentucky congressional delegation looks forward to meeting you in Washington this November. Come prepared for an exciting, invigorating week. These seven days may well serve as prologue to a life of significant contribution to your country and its enduring ideals.

Very Truly Yours,

Brock R. Martin
Secretary to Hon. John Sherman Cooper,
U. S. Senator, Commonwealth of Kentucky

Wednesday, December 25, 1963

Miss Claire Lyons
4212 Waterbury Street
New Haven 6, Connecticut

Dear Claire,
Merry Christmas, Tigger!
I searched for hours yesterday—pockets, books, billfold, the empty suitcase, everywhere—but I could not find that scrap of paper you wrote your address on. I finally did find it just now, and guess where? In my guitar case! Bright, huh? Anyhow, now that I found it, I'm using it. I promise not to wear it out. I intended on waiting longer before writing, but I really need to talk.

It is Christmas and the entire Menifee family and most of the Selbys and Satterfields are crammed into our small house. Dinner dishes were cleared not an hour ago, I am still stuffed, and already Grandma is filling a plate with ham and mustard sandwiches. There are cousins all over the house. My bed is buried under coats. So here I am in the hayloft, terrorizing the barn cats and writing to you.

I am so anxious for school to be over, summer done, and the rest of my life to begin. Berea College is nothing like Georgetown University. I know that. But it will be my first step out of here and into the world. Even before our week at the Youth Conference, I was eager to get going. Meeting and talking to others out there—people like you, people who are alive and bubbling with ideas and hope—has me primed.

As payback for the school district's funding my trip, I gave an oral report at assembly last Friday. Did you have to do that, too? If so, I'll bet that your classmates understood better, what with New Haven being a college town. I expect I did a decent enough job for those who cared to listen, but afterward most of the questions were simple-minded, quarrelsome, or downright dumb. For example: Will they cover the flame at President Kennedy's grave when it snows so it won't go out? Did I see Jacqueline, Caroline, and John-John? Do guards frisk the people who print the money before letting them go home at night? How come the Washington government wastes our tax money on big offices, fancy monuments, and foreign countries that side with the Communists anyway, while loyal Americans are going hungry and needing jobs? So now do you see why I want the heck out of here?

Travis Carter from up in Clark County came to the assembly and stayed on for supper with my folks. Travis is the youth delegate who had to cancel after they delayed the conference into December. Without that, I wouldn't have gone. The end of November we finally got rain after a dry summer and fall, and Travis's father kept him home to strip tobacco. He doesn't say anything against his father for holding him back, Claire, but you could see it in his eyes. After supper, he wanted to hear everything about the week, hour by hour. I told it all as best I could. But, as you know, being there was special. I guess I should feel grateful that his father did that, and I guess I do. At the same time, I feel bad that Travis missed out. He has applied to Berea College and should get in. We want to room together come fall, if they let us have a say in it.

Do you like this pen? I mean, do you like how it writes? It was under the tree this morning, a present from Uncle Harlan. It's a ballpoint, and the barrel is clear plastic so you can see how much ink is left. Hasn't smudged yet!

I guess I've rambled enough. I hope you will write back sometime, Claire. Can't say that I ever met anyone like you. I talked and laughed more in that week with you than I probably ever have. It's only seventeen days since the conference, and already I almost ache to talk with someone interesting and fun like you again.

Write when you can.

Your Pooh,

Davis Menifee

December 25, 1963

Davis Menifee, Jr.
Post Office Box #47
Colton Creek Rd.
Spivey, Kentucky

Hi, Davis,
My head is still swimming from the Youth Leadership Conference. Have you come down to earth yet? I haven't.

This morning I was counting up how many addresses I picked up, how many people I promised to write to (all people I *want* to keep in touch with), and do you know how many there are? Twenty-five! Imagine, meeting twenty-five truly interesting, new friends in a single week. Amazing. So I resolved to start today and to write to every last one of them in the next seven days. Since your name is in the middle of the alphabet, you are first. Ha ha!

Let me list the things I remember most, the things that impressed me most. When you write back, tell me which would be on your list and what things you would add.

Senator Dirksen's eyebrows (ha ha, only kidding!).
How clean they keep Washington (you should see New
York—filthy!).
Hundreds of government committees and meetings all going
on at the same time.
How incredibly somber we all were the first day because of
Kennedy.
How quickly the mood changed, once we mingled at lunch.
Morning fog rolling off the Potomac, blanketing the Jefferson
Memorial.
All those statues!
Feeling small.
Wanting the week to never end.
Group sings where we didn't have to worry about enunciation,
tonal clarity, or harmony (although we did happen on some
great accidental harmonies).

Your guitar playing. You said "Doc Watson." I thought "Bob Dylan." Either way, you have a talent, Pooh.

Congressmen addressing an empty chamber (which I personally find disgraceful!).

Pajama parties at the AU dorm where we talked about more than boys.

Popcorn at midnight, then waking up with greasy, salty fingers.

Being talked to like someone important.

Being listened to.

Suddenly realizing during Senator Margaret Chase Smith's talk that the young men and women in that room will be leading America someday soon. I mean, really realizing that as fact, not just words.

Sheets of money sliding out of printing presses faster than the eye can see, which makes you wonder why we can't cure poverty. If you cut through the economists' mumbo jumbo, all it takes is money. Right?

The Oval Office. I felt as if I was trespassing on a religious shrine. (Did you notice the dents in the carpet from Kennedy's furniture?)

A sickness in my stomach as the train left New Haven headed for Washington. Apprehension? Plain old homesickness? Diesel fumes? (Ha!)

A different emptiness inside boarding the train for the trip home. They told us the conference would be a beginning. In a way, it felt more like an end.

Those deplorable Negro slums between our dorm and Union Station.

The bright green strips of sod covering the gas line to Kennedy's grave. (No idea why I remember that.)

Zillions of tiny white Christmas lights covering every tree and bush on the mall.

Tigger and Pooh lying on their backs near the Washington Monument, talking streaks about themselves, laughing at nothing, and trying to find shapes in the clouds.

I could go on and on. But I guess you know that by now!

So how are things back home, Davis? Hope you are enjoying your Christmas Day. We had snow last night. Do you have snow?

Have you worked up your courage and had that talk with your father? I think I understand what you tried to tell me. In many ways, it is different for girls and their mothers. But maybe not as different as you think.

I imagine that you are busy with schoolwork and activities, as am I. But please do write back. I count you as a special friend, and I hope you always will be.

Sincerely,

Claire Lyons

Saturday, November 2, 1967

Claire Lyons
Room 220
Kraiger Hall West
Wellesley College
Wellesley, MA 02481

Dear Claire,
Yes, I received your September letter. Believe me, I intended to write back immediately, but things have been getting tense here. How do I excuse me? Let me count the ways:

Midterm exams. It is impossible to fake Chemistry, I learned. I've finally raised my grade back to B, and it was not easy. Surely, you will accept that excuse, Claire.

Trips home to visit Dad. Yes, his breathing problems have gotten worse. Thankfully, Mom is a pillar. She didn't even fuss about the length of my hair.

The Cause. Why continue the war? It is wrong. Dead wrong! How many thousands have we sacrificed already? How many more will we send there to die? And for what? Okay, I'm preaching to the choir. I know that, Claire. But sometimes it seems that the folks in the choir are the only ones who listen, the only ones who give a damn about this obscene war.

Roommate relocation. Travis Clark moved out last Tuesday. I suppose it was inevitable. We were a truly odd pairing, becoming odder by the month, he in his Army Reserve duds, and me wearing tie-dye. I will miss late-night debates with Travis. He has his moral blind spots, but his mind is keen, and that is more than I can say for the apathetic masses that inhabit this rural campus. Anyway, Travis's stuff is gone, and I've spread out to fill the whole room.

Music. My guitar picking is passable. My voice sucks. Some refuse to hear our message when we protest in the streets, but they just might take the medicine song-coated. Besides, most nights there is pot smoke wafting up from the front rows and I snag a free buzz. (Do not fret, dear heart. I am *not* heavy into drugs. But I do feel zoned out after forty-eight hours without sleep, which I do way too often.)

Anyway, those are my excuses. Accept them, please, Tigger? Enough about me.

Yale Law School? You must be psyched! I wasn't sure that closeting you away at Wellesley with thousands of other females would be such a good idea. But it does seem to have made for good study habits, judging from the way you have lived on the Dean's list. And look where all that hard work is landing you—right smack back in your old bed in New Haven. Or will you live on campus?

No need to rush to complete your law degree on my account, counselor. I plan to defend myself, if my draft-card-burning case ever does comes to trial. It is a federal offense, and the federal court dockets are overflowing. We are bringing the system to a halt with our disobedience, just like Gandhi did. My hearing has been postponed until at least next spring. They've got their page-one newspaper photos. That is Davis Menifee, plain as day, flaming card in hand. They must think they've got me. We will let the case come before a judge before we whip out the real card. I am no lawyer, but I'm pretty sure there are no laws against burning a copy, even an excellent copy. Am I right in that, counselor?

You asked about my plans for grad school next year. How can I say this gently? Impossible. I attend Berea College tuition-free. Turning out Appalachian woodcrafts fifteen hours a week pays some of my keep, but mostly it's a free ride. No, there will be no graduate school for me. I count myself lucky just getting these four years. It's my ticket out. Without that, my life would be tobacco or coal or both, like all the other Selbys and Menifees.

So I'll graduate in June and take my chances with the Burkitt County Draft Board. I suspect that old man Widicus already has his sights set on me. Probably looking forward to handing me the draft notice personally. May even be selling tickets to my first military haircut.

Be good. Be well. Be free.

Davis

November 14, 1967

Davis Menifee
Room 112
Fee Residence Hall
Berea, Kentucky 40403

Dear Davis,

Yes, I am thrilled about Yale. Of course, nothing is official yet, but my father's partner inquired, and it looks very promising. Yale has instituted opportunity-equalization plans to address previous underrepresentation of Blacks and women in the Law School. But from what he learned, my application is ranked high enough that I should make the cut, even without an affirmative action boost. All that midnight oil is paying off.

Closeted away? Good God, Davis! What gave you that idea? You will be pleased to know that a woman here at Wellesley has as many dates as she wants. The streets are filled with Harvard lads and other assorted ne'er-do-wells who would gladly bed a cerebral woman so they can brag to their buddies the next morning. Not counting that one ill-considered choice I made as a dewy-eyed sophomore, I have managed to avoid them all. Men can be such distractions to a woman with a plan, after all. But thank you for your most solicitous expression of concern, my Pooh.

Sometimes I sound snooty. I know that. Please don't misinterpret my question about grad school. I just know that you have so few options regarding the draft, and I would hate for you, of all people, to have to go. I listen to the news each evening. Some days it does sound hopeful. We are doing what we can here in Boston. I just want this war to be over before you get called.

I smelled tear gas last weekend. No, it was not directed at us. We were sitting on the sidewalk in front of the Suffolk County Draft Board. I had brokered a deal with the local police whereby we would remain silent, hold handmade signs without sticks, and allow recruits to pass unmolested through our line. The commitment was contingent on the police not interfering with our legal right to demonstrate. Not a bad deal for our side, because we had all three Boston television stations out there videotaping. Frank Bourko from BU, George Everett from Harvard, and I were interviewed by a mostly sympathetic press. My greatest hope is that print and broadcast media bring all their influence to this issue and that the American people, at last, understand that Johnson has taken our foreign policy in a very wrong direction.

Sitting on that sidewalk, I looked up at the faces of those young men, Davis, and it scared me. They are so young, most of them younger than you and I. I could almost smell their fear. They will never know it, but I said a silent prayer for each one of them. Brassy of me, considering that I haven't attended church since turning twelve. But if there is a God, surely He must respect a worthy prayer, regardless of where it originates. Besides, it never hurts to hedge your bets in these matters.

The tear gas—that was directed at a splinter group. I didn't recognize them. They marched up to the courthouse entrance, chained the doors, and tried to hole up in the entryway. I caught one nauseating whiff and almost gave up lunch. My eyes teared up and stayed red through Sunday. I still can't wear my contact lenses.

No, I won't have my law degree in time to help you with your case, Davis. Please don't be too confident that some arcane law from the 1800s won't be pulled from their judicial hats to charge you. Be careful. I do appreciate the vote of confidence in my fledgling legal skills. Seriously, I can ask my father to make some inquiries within the legal community in New England. They are bound to have contacts down there who can help, if your case does come before a judge.

There are options to the draft, I'm sure you know, besides ducking into graduate school. Community service is an option, but I think you have to have a recognized religion behind you to validate your objector status. Just don't go shooting your big toe off in some convenient hunting accident, Davis. (It's a joke. Smile; damn it!) And please don't leave the country, unless you are left with absolutely no option.

I know hundreds of war objectors here, and none is more solid in his convictions, more conscientious than you, dear Pooh. Whatever path you choose, I could never judge you harshly. We shared those seven days in December what seems like eons ago (was it only four years?), and you have never been far from my thoughts since. You have a brave heart and an innocent soul. I do so wish there were some way I could help.

Be good. Be well. Be free, yourself.

Claire

Sunday, July 4, 1971

Ms. Claire Lyons
644-1/2 West Boynton St.
Hartford, CT 06151

Dear Claire,
Congratulations on passing the bar exam. I am so proud of you! Have you hung out your shingle? If so, please send a photograph, and include one of Hartford's newest lawyer while you are at it. My most recent Claire photo dates to circa 1966. In it you are all braids and flowers. Surely, you wear neat suits now and have your hair clipped in a fashion more appropriate to your chosen profession. Show me, please?

Strange, but when I think of you at Yale, I don't imagine that young woman in the photograph. I still see the girl I met in DC seven years ago. If some day you walked by me on a street here in

Toronto, would I recognize you? Yes, I think I would, but there might be an instant when I would think that perhaps you are the older sister of the girl I remember.

The baby gift is perfect. Who but you would send a golden fleece for our little Jason? The significance was lost on Rachel, unfortunately, but I appreciated it enough for both of us.

Two months into life, and my son does not understand that nights are for sleeping. He is about to drive his mother crazy. I'm still working nights at the radio station, so she is the one left to cope with his nighttime crankiness. I worry that she is losing patience.

I have discovered something very interesting about being an expatriate antiwar protestor. The Canadian citizenry could not care less about what those fools south of the border are doing in Southeast Asia. I couldn't get a decent protest organized if I promised them Dylan, Baez, and Fonda would all show up. And the United States government—president, congressmen, everyone— they all ignore written appeals to reason. If you are not in their collective face, actively protesting and disrupting, they act as if you don't exist. And now that I am a fugitive from their version of justice, I clearly am of no concern. Frankly, I believe that they are glad to be rid of me—me and the other tens of thousands who made the same choice of conscience.

Now that I am back in Toronto, I will tell you that I made a quick foray into the States last month. Yes, I trust you, Claire, but I do not trust Uncle Sammy to respect the sanctity of his citizens' mail. I went to finally say my good-byes to Dad. It has been most of a year, but until recently, I didn't have a safe way across the border and back.

Felt strange, standing at my father's grave. I felt grief, but also relief for him. I remember Dad coming home from the mine after working long hours, his white eyes staring out from a dust-covered face, its wrinkles lined black with a slurry of sweat and powder coal, his ears black outside and in. The palms of his hands were callused and his knuckles scabbed. The coal was worked so deep into the hide on the back of his hands that I doubted it would ever come out. I often wondered if Appalachian morticians have a special potion for the faces and hands of coal-miner corpses, some- thing that magically erases the evidence of a life spent laboring underground, something that purifies their skin for a neat coffin showing before sending them back underground.

He did not have a bad life, my father. He had the life he was raised for, the life he chose in many ways. There were angry words between us years ago, words about that life, words I would take back if I could. They are gone now, dried up and blown away like last year's leaves. I think he understood, and maybe he forgave. I hope so.

One image of my father haunts me. I hoped to exorcise it by going back for a final good-bye. At times he had a particular look in his eyes, a vacant stare soaked through with despair. The look was strangely familiar, but for the longest time I could not put a finger on where I had seen it. Then one morning when I was fifteen I woke up knowing. It was the dull stare of my Great-grandfather Satterfield's plow mule—exhaustion, stultifying sameness, dull pain that abides everywhere and always. Some mornings, after breakfast and before the sun was full up, while Mom packed his lunch pail, Dad rocked on the front porch and smoked his morning pipe. I would see that tired mule look envelop him. As I write about it now, I shudder.

Mom is doing okay. Life goes on, she says. She scolded me like a seven-year-old for not bringing Rachel and her new grandbaby along. The fact that I am a fugitive doesn't seem to register with her, and that is probably just as well.

My youngest brother, Phil, was discharged from the Marines in May. He is scraping together money to buy into a car repair business in Somerset. I offered to pitch in the few dollars I could spare, but he said he'd sooner drink spit. Phil knows how to make his point. Then he added that I should count myself lucky he had kept his mouth shut about my sneaking back into the country. It had not occurred to me that he might go against family. I doubt he would, but I left Spivey that night, anyway.

Let me correct something that I wrote before, about Rachel's losing patience. She is really an excellent mother. I could never do what she does. You might think us a strange pair, Claire, knowing me as you do. She is very different from me—settled, domestic, quite orderly, and romantic in her own structured way. As you well know, I am none of these. Still, we seem to mesh quite well, her making up for some of my shortcomings, and me adding a dash or two of danger and unpredictability to her otherwise settled lifestyle. She enjoys introducing her long-haired American expatriate around to her sizable extended family, her friends, and various acquaintances. And maybe I get off on playing the mysterious and possibly dangerous outsider.

I'm afraid this letter has turned out to be more about me than I had intended. Do write back soon, Claire, and tell me about hanging your shingle, about your plans, and what lies ahead. And don't forget that picture.

As always,

Davis

———

July 10, 1971

Davis Menifee
2221 Queens Blvd. West
Toronto, Ontario
M1N 3C2

Dear Davis,
My shingle hangs in a storefront on Hartford's riverfront. It is painted in letters large enough to be seen by passing cars. Women's Legal Resource. Free Legal Services for Women in Need. Look at it this way: I come to work in jeans and thereby save several thousand dollars every year in wardrobe costs, all of which I plow back into hiring local women as typing and filing help, which lets me serve more clients. Pictures enclosed, as requested. One hint: I'm the frizzy-haired white girl on the right, just in case you are still looking for that naive young preppy you met in Washington, D.C.

Feeling guilty? Good! Now I'll ease you off the hook. Until three months ago, I expected to buy the suits and sign on with one of Connecticut's better law firms. The interviews went well, and there would have been job offers. I am certain of that. But there was one moment when the old boys were recruiting me, and I realized that their recruiting had little to do with me as a person. And it was not just a quota issue, although there was some of that. The fact is they were interested in what they could turn me into, not in who I was. No one asked about what causes I cared most about, what cases I could bring the most passion to, what flames burned in me that they could use to help their clients. It was never about me. It was about them and the firm. I'm not ready to give myself up to that.

The woman on the left in the group photo is Celeste Jefferson. She passed the bar two years ago and has been making a difference in this neighborhood since then. The challenges are two: first, funding for legal research and clerical help, and second, finding enough hours in the day for all the women who need help. I can help with the first by tapping into folks with more money than they can reasonably use. And the second is just a question of commitment, and I am deeply committed to helping these women. They are the victims of landlords, husbands, boyfriends, and sometimes the legal system itself. Celeste has been going to bat for them. Now I do, too.

Now that you see a recent picture, answer your own question honestly. Would you walk past? Would you think I'm an older sister? Or maybe you would make a pass at me? Oh, that's right. You are a married man now! Scratch that last question.

So tell me more about this young terror, this Jason of yours. Does he have your devilish eyes? How about some photographic retribution, Davis. I'd like a picture of father and son. Wife, too, if she is not serving as shutter clicker.

War protests continue here in Hartford and New Haven, but much of the early passion has dissipated. The movement's new leadership is too slick, their speeches too cool. I wonder what happened to the fire. The war still goes on. More young men die every day. It should matter. After so many years of killing and death, maybe we are all a little numb.

I'm funneling my energy into women's issues, an area where I can make a real difference. At the end of the day, I can point to things I did that made the life of some woman better. That is extremely gratifying. After banging my head against the pro-war forces for so long and getting absolutely nowhere, every bit of progress feels like a major advance.

Please never apologize for filling your letters with yourself, Davis. If I do not allow you that, how can I, in good conscience, inflict on you my tales of The Incredible Claire Lyons, personal savior of all womankind? This peculiar relationship of ours will not long endure unless we allow each other ever-increasing ego room. I shall do my part, and only hope that you will do yours.

Do not forget! Send family pictures!

Yours always,

Claire Lyons

Tuesday, December 23, 1975

Ms. Claire King
4911 Fairway Drive
West Hartford, CT 06104

Dear Claire,

Rachel and I want to thank you for the Christmas card and terrific note. Sounds like you and Nolan really enjoyed your first year of marriage. And judging from your ripeness in that standard fireplace picture, I'd say you are positively glowing. (You *are* pregnant, aren't you? God, I'll be absolutely mortified if you are not.)

You asked about what we planned, now that Ford has declared amnesty for us criminals. It is hard to say, Claire. Naturally, Rachel and I talked it through before we married. What I said at that point—and it was true then, more so than now—is that I didn't have any objection to living out my life here in Canada, if that's what my future had to be. Hell, I made that choice the day I crossed the border. But things have changed over the years. And things haven't worked out like I expected in many ways.

Thousands of us came to Canada in those years. I expected that we would form a loyal, expatriate community—still loving our country, but opposed to a wrong-minded war waged by a government that had usurped all power from its people. Sad to say, we are less a community than I expected. Some of us did try to unite, to become a cohesive influence for peace, to function as a legitimate, loyal opposition to an errant regime in Washington. But most expats soon turned bitter. They still live in enclaves, some in the cities, some in suburbs, and the remainder scattered across the provinces on cooperative farms and remnant communes. Walk into any Toronto bar featuring televised American baseball, and you will see them still, downing their beers and exchanging vitriol about their lots in life. Canadians generally hold us in low regard. We are, after all, a pretty sorry lot, taken as a whole.

Now that an amnesty has been declared, Rachel and I have discussed it again, several times, at length, and loudly. You might say that we have argued. Okay, we *have* argued. I feel strange telling you this, as if I am breaking an unspoken marriage vow. Ye shall not discuss family matters outside the family. Is that how it goes? I have never seen it written down, but it is ingrained in me as deeply as the Ten Commandments.

If it were a simple question—live in Canada near her family or return to the States and live nearer mine—I could go either way and be content. But the sad fact is that I am a second-class citizen here in Canada. I see it in how people look at me when they learn where I come from and guess why I'm here. Earlier this year when they needed to reduce expenses at the radio station, my hours were the ones cut. No one said why, but I know.

Rachel thinks this is all in my head. I just know that I don't want to go through life feeling second-class, and that is how I feel here. Maybe that perception is right on, and maybe it is dead wrong. In the final analysis, it doesn't really matter. You can understand that, can't you, Claire? Rachel doesn't. She says I'm imagining slights that aren't there. Doesn't matter, I tell her. Hurts the same, either way.

And then there is our son. Jason complicates the equation even more.

Well, now I *am* sorry. You send a lovely Christmas card and newsy note, and you get three buckets of gloom back from me. Sometimes I wonder why you continue to write. But then I remember. It's my devilish eyes.

Keep the faith, Claire. We will all come out smiling on the other side.

Your ever faithful,

Davis

December 28, 1975

Davis Menifee
2221 Queens Blvd. West
Toronto, Ontario
M1N 3C2

Dear Davis,
First of all, you need not feel mortified. Nolan and I are expecting our first child in mid-March. Tests indicate that we should paint blue. We are still open for suggestions regarding first and middle names appropriate to males. Certain names that may come to mind will, I warn you, be rejected summarily.

I recognize the very human hesitancy to share matters of the clan outside the clan. And I treasure that, in the face of that force, you shared a confidence with me. I have no advice to offer, no help to give. But please know that there is a ready ear and a caring heart here in Connecticut. And far from spreading gloom on my Christmas, you have transformed it into a most special one.

Now, on a brighter note: Do you remember meeting Congressman Westover in Washington during the 1963 Youth Leadership Conference? For the past year, I have been working with him on legislation to equalize women's access to the legal system. He wants me to consider running for the Connecticut House of Representatives. Can you believe it, Davis, me in politics? One minute it seems like pure fantasy and the next I find myself writing lists of all we could accomplish if we got this state's government pulling in the right direction. Imagine what a difference we could

make. Nolan has been surprisingly equivocal. Celeste says, "Go!"
I just might give it a try. Tell me what you think.

> Your friend,
>
> Claire

Sunday, December 2, 1979

Ms. Claire King
12 Westwood Lane
West Hartford, CT 06122

Dear Claire,

You have ruined me but good, Claire King, with your thought-
ful birthday gift, and I do love you for it. After a solid week of
listening to that Doc Watson album, I had to get my hands around
a guitar again. I shopped the local pawnshops and found a vintage
Gibson B25 acoustic with two stripped tuners, which I have
replaced. After some tender refinishing, she is almost as good as
new. I gave her a final varnish coat this afternoon. She is drying
in the basement right now. My fingers have forgotten most of
what they knew, they don't spread like they did, and I have lost
strength in my left hand. But that will return in time. I have warned
Rachel that the sounds we will make getting back into practice
won't be very pleasant.

We noticed immediately that the sound of the guitar calms
Jason. Records, even ol' Doc Watson's, don't have the same effect.
The Gibson helps settle him in the evenings, before his bedtime
dose. His doctor swears that he will outgrow this, that we can
withdraw him from the medication as his system matures. I just
hate seeing him fogged out. But Rachel can't take his frenzies
when he isn't medicated. Not sure I could either, after a few days.

I have a new job title—Catalyst Specialist. Little fatter paycheck
comes along with it. Mom says she's glad I'm finally making that
chemistry degree pay off. She still nags us to visit more often, so

she can hug her "foreigner grandbaby." But travel with Jason is a challenge, to say the least. Once a year is all that Rachel can tolerate.

I took Jason to Perkins Shore Park this morning to fly kites and run off his energy. What a rare December morning it was for Toronto. The sun reflected low off the water. The frozen ground, warmed by a glorious breeze up from the south, softened the earth to grassy mud beneath the soles of our shoes. The earth's aroma floated up. I closed my eyes and was carried back to planting time in Spivey. Strange, what smells trigger in the brain. I wished I had brought my guitar along. Next time, the weather will be too cold. Stays cold here well into May.

Write when you have a chance. I know you are busy with everything, but I do so enjoy hearing from you. My best to Nolan, Andrew, and little Kayla.

Davis

December 8, 1979

Davis Menifee
2221 Queens Blvd. West
Toronto, Ontario
M1N 3C2

Dear Davis,
Six weeks after hurricane Francine, and Connecticut is still struggling to get life back to normal. Hartford escaped relatively unscathed. South of here, along the coast, hundreds of people lost everything to the flooding. For the past few weeks I've been shuttling between Hartford and Washington, begging, cajoling, and bargaining with whatever political currency I have to get these people the relief they need. Everyone wants to forget after two weeks, once the reporters pack up and go home. For the victims, the battle to get back on their feet is just starting. Nolan's church will do what they can for Christmas, especially for the children, but we know that it will be dreadful for them.

On the home front, Andrew is sprouting up. My husband thinks that he may have fathered the next Bill Walton. I'm thinking maybe a dancer, the next Tommy Tune, perhaps. Time will tell. Our darling Kayla babbles constantly, smiles, and fills her diaper regularly. Nolan says she takes after me. Ha!

The new house hasn't started to feel like home yet. Boxes unpacked, pictures hung, books all neatly shelved. I still make wrong turns sometimes going from room to room. I feel like a research rat in a maze experiment, one where the psychologist moves the walls around and clocks how long it takes you to learn the new path to your food morsel. Are we getting older, or are our brains finally getting full?

Nolan has left the bank. He will head up the local office of a major institutional investment firm. He also has gotten himself appointed to the Greater Hartford Industrial Development Commission. Do I sound proud? I am. Of course, it means that I am hosting still more dinner parties. Until last year, I was preparing the food for these soirees myself, but there are not enough hours in my day anymore. The catering services love me, but I swear that I will gag if I see another little weenie on a toothpick.

Glad you are enjoying the record album. I saw it in the window of a secondhand shop several months ago and nearly jumped out of my skin. Hubby thought I'd gone absolutely berserk. After I bought it, I worried that maybe you had the record already. But I figured that, if you did, you would probably have worn it out by now and could use a replacement anyway. It has been wrapped and sitting in a corner of my office for what felt like forever. I wish I could have seen you open it. If it inspired you to go out and buy a guitar, great! I didn't know whether or not you still play. You hadn't mentioned it. I guess I imagined that you still did, maybe for your own pleasure. In any case, it delights me to hear that you are back at it. Once your fingers are fully functional again, please tune up your singing voice, Davis. You never seemed to appreciate its uniqueness. I did. But then again, I was an unworldly young thing, easily impressed by a handsome young man who brought his guitar to Washington.

Wishing you only the best,

Claire

Saturday, December 19, 1987

Hon. Claire King
2212 Georgetown Place East
Washington, D.C. 20057

Dear Claire,

Thank you for your card and your kind words of concern for Jason, Rachel, and me. They mean more than you can know.

Our son is scheduled to finish his rehab in another ten days. His counselor tells us that he is giving it a stronger effort this time. He assured us that Jason can live drug-free, if he makes the decision and sticks with it. How we hope he does.

Yes, this has been painful for me, but less so than for Rachel. She relates his current drug problems to the hyperactivity medication he was prescribed when he was young. Should she have put up with his misbehaving more, left the pills in the bottle, taken him to run off his energy in the park instead? Should she have turned a deaf ear to the teachers who encouraged her to increase his dosage for the sake of his classmates? Rachel takes on guilt readily, and Jason's situation has created plenty. Couple that with her inordinate fear of AIDS—yes, Jason used IV drugs this time—and there are days when the combination of guilt and fear overwhelms her. Some days it is all that I can do to keep her from sinking.

I cannot begin to imagine how difficult this is for Jason. The boy has always held his feelings close. His counselor tells me, "He will get better and stay drug-free, but only if that is his choice." Easy for him to say. Jason is just one of hundreds to him. But this is my son, my only child. When we talk at the rehab center, I look into Jason's eyes, eyes that mirror my own, and I see a clear plea for help there, a plea that he cannot bring himself to voice. So what do I do? If rehab isn't enough, then what is? The questions keep me awake at night.

I've been meaning to ask, Madame Congressperson: Since moving to Georgetown, have you walked past that place near the Washington Monument where we first talked and sought the wisdom of clouds? Someday I hope I get back to DC, if only to revisit that place. Silly, I suppose. While I am in town, I just might stop off at the Capitol building to see Madame Congressperson, too.

We received a phone call from Mom yesterday, her first call to Canada since Dad died. She is well and looking forward to moving to Florida. Phil is opening an oil-change franchise in Kissimmee, and he's taking her along. I didn't think he could get her out of Kentucky with dynamite. Shows what I know.

Mom and I talked for quite a while. It felt so comforting, especially with the turmoil surrounding Jason. When I asked her about missing home, she said that the place she thought of as home had always been Grandpa Satterfield's cabin on Licking River. She lived there as a young girl. She has been gone from that place for many years. In the 1960s they dug up her people's graves, the ones they could find, and removed them to high ground. Then they dammed up the Licking. She recounted watching from the hill above the sawmill that fall as her home slowly slipped beneath the rising surface of what would become Cave Run Lake. First the old homestead flooded; then the graveyard, the apple orchard, and eventually the sawmill and the woods halfway up to Turner Ridge. Every summer thereafter, around mid-June, she'd rent herself a rowboat, put out on that lake, and try to reckon her way over top of the old place, based on her memory of distant hills to the south and east. Seems unlikely that she always found the right spot, but she swears that she did. She would set a line deep in the water right there. Phil called her daft, fishing the middle when everyone knows fish stay amongst the sunken trees close to shore. She claims to have caught at least a catfish and sometimes a muskie in that spot every year. She said that it was a special fish, a fish that had slept in her old bed. She took great delight in pan-frying and eating that special fish herself. She plans to have Phil drive her back to Cave Run Lake each year, come mid-June, for a little fishing. If he does that, she won't feel farther from home in Kissimmee than she did most days in Spivey.

I have played a few gigs at a local nightclub. Actually, it is a country and western bar more than a nightclub. Tuesday night is folk night. The owner opens up the mike to any fool with a banjo, guitar, or harmonica and blind courage. His club doesn't have chicken wire between patrons and stage, like in the States. At least in this regard, Canadians are more civilized. I'm not very good, but it gets me out once a week and lets me be someone else for a while.

Work at the refinery is the same. I'm doing okay, but no better than that. I check the newspaper ads for something else. I need a change.

Write when time allows. Tell me how you and the kids are doing, Claire. I do love hearing from you.

Davis

December 26, 1987

Davis Menifee
2221 Queens Blvd. West
Toronto, Ontario
M1N 3C2

Dear Davis,
Our thoughts are with Jason as he works his way through rehab, and with you and Rachel as you sort through your issues.

So my favorite troubadour is back on stage, entertaining another generation of radicals. Fabulous! Are you doing those great songs from the sixties, something popular today, or have you started writing again? I would love to hear you sing again, Davis. Please record a tape for me some evening. I would truly treasure it.

I pass by the Washington Monument several times a week, Davis, rushing to one place or another. But I always pause at our spot on the grass. I wonder if I remember it right. I have it firmly planted in my mind that we stretched out about fifty feet off the northwest corner of the monument, partway down the slope. But I could be wrong. After all these years, I think maybe I am remembering the memory and not the day itself. That said, the sound-bite answer to your question is this: Yes, I remember, and it makes me smile.

Update on the King Clan: Andrew has stopped missing his old buddies in Connecticut and is deeply involved with Boy Scouts, youth league basketball, and a leggy cheerleader named Tanya. Kayla stills smiles a lot, but she misses her Daddy back in Connecticut and requires a larger allotment of hugs and bedtime snuggling. Little Ben started preschool without a hitch. He seems not to notice that this isn't Connecticut and his father isn't upstairs.

Claire King is doing the best that she can. Now that I'm here, I feel as if there's so much I want to accomplish. But there are obstacles. Years ago you wrote that you felt like an outsider in Canada, as if you were somehow second-class. I think I am getting a dose of the same from my new colleagues here in the House. Their smiles are broad, and their handshakes are firm. But I was appointed, not elected, and that carries a stigma in this town. I plan to run and win, but until I do, I reside on the bottom of their precious totem pole. Still, I have a vote and I use it. And I have a voice to speak. The fact that the chamber is empty is unimportant. The power is in what the television camera captures, in what the networks send over the airwaves, not in whether or not my colleagues' butts are in their House chamber chairs. Those old men keep their collective fingers on that electronic pulse, believe me. Get on the nightly news. Then they'll hear and heed you.

Nolan and I are learning that separation can be a relief. If I am elected to a full House term, and that *is* my firm intention, we may well make it permanent. If I lose, we will have to determine which of our options is best for all concerned. As things stand now, the kids are transitioning into a one-parent family rather painlessly. I know it won't be that simple, but I'm confident we'll all be okay.

You asked how my life is here in DC. It is frantic, to be honest. I don't know when or if the pace will slacken. As an appointed representative, I don't get the plum committee assignments. I get the drudge ones. You have no idea the hours I put in, the endless meetings and the hearings. On top of all that, Nolan's old cronies from his days with the Greater Hartford Industrial Development Commission phone me frequently with these little requests, most of which I carefully sidestep. I try to get back to Connecticut at least twice each month to stroke the politicos there. Sometimes I schedule two lunches for the same day, an early one with ostensible allies and a late one with blatant, backslapping enemies.

I haven't seen the inside of a gym since moving here. Last week, Celeste said, "Girlfriend, you are gaining weight." No shit!

My analyst tells me to slow down. "You try to do everything," she says. "Take some time to smell the roses." Hundred dollars an hour and I get sappy advice ripped off from seventies song lyrics. Poor woman doesn't realize she is dealing with a daughter of the sixties. We *can* have it all if we want, do it all if we take a mind to, and still find time to sniff whatever foliage we damn well please. Sure, the pace is frantic, but that just helps weed out the weak, the lame, the halfhearted. Those left standing are the truly passionate ones, the ones who work the hardest, strategically link themselves, and know when to press, when to compromise, and when to judiciously fade into the woodwork. Political Darwinism in DC does not favor the perpetuation of rose-smelling species.

Okay, I do find an occasional oasis for my soul—a warm bath, a bedtime story with Kayla, or a letter from my dearest friend.

Claire

Wednesday, March 13, 1991

Hon. Claire King
2212 Georgetown Place East
Washington, D.C. 20057

Dear Claire,
If you need a good laugh today, I may have one for you. Made me laugh, and that was a most welcome relief after so many months of total frustration and helplessness.

It seems that your favorite expatriate radical is being vigorously recruited to serve the jingoistic, military policies of my adopted country, as hip-joined ally of my forsaken one. I thought my first "no" was emphatic enough.

According to my corporate employer, our combined governments, and quite possibly my beloved Rachel, a new duty calls. Flaming Saudi oil wells and bombed refineries now demand that all patriotic oil men in the western hemisphere (most especially catalyst specialists) uproot from their self-centered lives, immediately board military aircraft, and travel halfway around the world to clean up this most recent mess. My answer is, "You broke them, you fix them." You have read my views on the politics of oil, Claire, more often than you've wanted, I suspect. Bush and his cronies want to rule the world's oil fields. They suckered kid brother Canada into tagging along. This is their mess. Let them clean it up. I will not lift one finger to help, no matter how much cash they wave beneath my nose.

Rachel says I'm a fool not to take their money. Her logic is that the fires will be extinguished, the wells capped, and the precious refineries rebuilt, regardless of whether I go or not. "Six months over there," she says, "and you could dig us out of twenty years of debt. We can finally get a few of the niceties of life, things we deserve." Okay, I can understand a little greed. I've been known to money-grub myself, on rare occasions. But then she says something that really bothers me. "They wouldn't ask you to go if it wasn't safe."

This is not about my safety, Claire, and it never has been, not now and not back then. Can she possibly believe for one second that my stands against war are based on anything but principle? Yes, some men came to Canada to save their hides from the Vietcong. Some had no politics other than survival. I didn't care then, and I don't care now. Not supporting war was the *right* choice, whatever their reasons. But what really bothers me is that Rachel, the woman I've lived with for more than twenty years, questions whether I am the principled man I claim to be or just a coward masquerading as one. The question never surfaced before. But now that money—big money to us—is involved, it has. Maybe it was always there in the back of her mind.

Admit it. Didn't you laugh, or at least smile, at the thought of your favorite conscientious objector, anti-imperialist, folk-singing catalyst specialist being enticed by the warmongers of the Western world into cleaning up their latest mess?

I do forgive you that war vote, Madame Congressperson. Politically fatal, totally empty gestures are unnecessary and probably stupid. A naked nay vote would have been just that. I am realist enough to grant you that. In your shoes, my choice would have-been an abstention. But I can only guess at the pressures you face.

Finally, do you have any update concerning Jason? I hate to pester on the subject, but we feel totally powerless, and all our other avenues have yielded nothing. You cannot imagine our absolute frustration.

Peace,

Davis

March 27, 1991

Davis Menifee
2221 Queens Blvd. West
Toronto, Ontario
M1N 3C2

Dear Davis,
You may not approve of my votes on Iraq, but please know that they were not cast without considerable thought. Once assurances were given regarding the full participation of female members of the military, I was comfortable casting my votes as I did. Without compelling reasons, it is best not to find yourself on the wrong side of a lopsided vote like this.

Celeste has agreed to stay on as my administrative assistant for one more term, thank God. I don't know what I would do without the woman. She is my one true friend and ally here, my rock, day in and day out.

I called around this morning for any new information regarding the search for Jason. My sources had nothing new to report. He did not enter the United States, at least not at a legal crossing point. CIA and FBI inquiries have turned up no trace of him. Unofficial contacts in Quebec City have yielded no news. There are no guarantees, of course, but in light of his background, the consensus view is that Jason is not a victim of foul play. The most likely scenario is the one you put forward in the beginning, that he has assumed another identity and is living anonymously, most probably somewhere in Canada. They will continue trying to locate your son, Davis, but frankly they feel that he will not be found until he decides to be.

There is no way for me to imagine how difficult this must be for Rachel and you. I try to imagine my Andrew beyond reach for months on end, but what I imagine must be only a fraction of your pain and frustration. I wish I could do more. But I am powerless, too.

Now I must ask a favor, Davis, and I hate that I must. Please try to understand, and *do not* take this personally. I am having an impact here in Washington. Among other things, that means that I am developing enemies. It comes from doing my job well. You can't pussyfoot here. You want something done, you go after it, and you step on toes. There is no avoiding it. Party labels tell only a part of the story. There are factions and feuds, and sometimes you find yourself a pawn in a chess game you don't even know is being played.

Enough of the rationale. Here is my request: please address your letters to me through Celeste. God, I feel so scummy even asking it, Davis. Please try to understand.

I can explain away old *Boston Globe* photos of young Claire Lyons picketing the Suffolk County Draft Board, if they surface, and I have little doubt that they will. I was young, idealistic, trying to do what was best for my country. Liberals will love it, and moderates can accept it, and conservatives—well, they don't vote for me, anyway. On the other hand, corresponding with you involves political risk. The tabloids love this stuff and, once exposed, things could get nasty. I know that it should not be this way, but it is. You are no criminal. You are one of thousands who tried to do what was right in difficult times. You acted with a pure conscience. But I think you can see, Davis, that the political effect on me could be quite bad if you and I are linked. Congress is stacked against us on this, with former POW's, Vietnam-era medal winners, and plenty of quasi-legal draft evaders who don't want their behinds held to that political fire ever again. Just let them catch one whiff of a draft dodger or, worse yet, a draft-card burner. My enemies will attack. My allies will dive for cover. Campaign contributions will dry up, and Claire King's tender, young political carcass will be fried.

Maybe I am paranoid about this. I don't know. But I am not ready to risk what we have started, and all that we might accomplish, by getting careless. So for now, until we can find a more workable way, Davis, please address your letters through Celeste at 314 Bordeen Place, Chevy Chase, MD 20825.

And now I think I'll go take a bath.

Claire

Saturday, November 22, 1997

Hon. Claire King
2212 Georgetown Place East
Washington, D.C. 20057

Dear Claire,

Nolan's dealings made page two of today's Toronto newspaper, so I suppose the story is all over your papers in the States. IPO shenanigans and commission kickbacks—not sure exactly what all those allegations mean, but I would guess that they will land your ex-husband in deep trouble. Nolan's mess won't splatter on you, I trust.

A package accompanies this letter—if Celeste didn't swipe it. You most probably opened it first, even before my letter. You may already be listening to it, if you guessed that the unmarked CD has music on it, not some computer game. You will hear selections from several artists, all recorded at my club over the past year. Even the incomparable Davis Menifee is there, picking and rasping his way through a self-penned effort. Tentatively track number eight on this first-burn version—skip to it if you must, but you will miss some truly fine music if you do. I play backup on two other tracks. The jewel case is temporary. Cardboard packaging, recyclable naturally, arrives from the printer the first week of December.

A glimmer of hope: Over the past few weeks, I've received five hang-up phone calls at the apartment. It is a new listing, so yes, it *could* be someone looking for the person who had the number before. Rachel and her new husband also received two similar calls. We think that it could be Jason. We want to believe it is.

Today, like every November twenty-second, Kennedy's assassination is mentioned on Toronto news broadcasts. Reporters ask people how they heard and where they were. Do you remember, Claire? I do. I was stuck in Spivey, and Burkitt County was in the midst of a drought. Fires burned in the hills for weeks. The bus to the 1963 Youth Leadership Conference had departed for Washington, and I moped my way through morning classes. Senator Cooper's letter was pressed in my notebook. No delegate had taken sick. I lamented that my life would never reach its promised prologue, let alone chapter one. During calculus class, Mr. Yarborough was called into the hall. When he returned he said that the president had been shot and we should all go home. I assumed that Kennedy was in Washington, and I remember wondering if anyone from Kentucky had been shot, too. When I got home, I heard that it happened in Dallas and Kennedy was dead. The day of his funeral, rain began falling in Spivey at long last. On television, I saw people my age along the funeral procession route, and I wondered if any were Youth Conference delegates. Then the phone rang, and I learned that the conference was postponed to next week because of the tragedy. A boy from Clark County had just canceled, they told me. Could I take his place? Rain was still falling four days later as I boarded the bus.

I will be flying to Florida for Thanksgiving. Mom worries that her single son needs a good meal. She will also show me off to members of her mahjong clique, I suspect. While I am in town, she wants me to meet someone named Harold. Phil worries that the guy is a gold digger, but I don't believe our mother owns so much as an ounce of gold, teeth included. Obladi. Oblada.

Hope you and the kids enjoy your Thanksgiving together.

Davis

November 27, 1997

Davis Menifee
44 West Seventeenth Ave. Apt 1E
Toronto, Ontario
M6N 1R1

Dear Davis,

I know how much you want those phone calls to be from your son. I truly hope that they are. Or they may be wrong numbers, as you said. Can you get caller ID on your phone? Or would you rather not dash the hope?

The CD is truly treasured, Davis. When you become famous, I shall amaze my friends with tales of knowing you when you were but a Kentucky farm boy, and I shall take credit for coaxing you into picking up a guitar again. Now tell me, would you find me a table, Davis, if I just showed up some evening at your club?

Yes, Nolan's problems are substantial and inescapable, I'm afraid. I feel sorry for him, because he was duped. Yes, he was greedy, greedy for a couple million, not the hundred million plus in press reports. Yes, he knew what he was doing was illegal. It wasn't his scheme, but the blame may stop with him. Nolan is in a box, and he'd sooner serve thirty years than name certain names. He will develop serious health concerns if he talks. So those who hatched the scheme and who will end up with the bulk of the cash will probably never be named.

Sad to say, Nolan's problems damage me quite seriously. Politically speaking, I would say that my wounds will prove fatal.

We are separated, not divorced. It seemed like a reasonable convenience at the time. I avoided alienating my Catholic constituency, and he was free to roam. We have been essentially divorced for a decade. But it is a long way from essentially to actually, as any tabloid reporter worth her ink will tell you. By this weekend, I expect to be widely known as Claire King, Connecticut Congresswoman and estranged wife of accused stock manipulator Nolan King, who was recently arraigned on twenty-seven counts of securities fraud. Once the tabloids link me with the story, the more respectable dailies and broadcast media will follow, and then there will be nothing we can do to make it go away.

Before this past Monday, I hadn't talked to Nolan in almost three years. No court will accuse or convict me of one damned thing. Nevertheless, I am politically dead.

Campaign funding promises are being quickly withdrawn. The party whip wants a meeting. Intermediaries indicate that he will encourage me to formulate exit strategies and consider options for alternate avenues for public service. I've floated the idea of a full professorship at Georgetown. How does that sound, Davis?

Celeste, bless her heart, has held reporters at bay thus far. We are discussing how best to get my story out. Television is quickest, the most direct. We won't go on live, though; they can ambush you live. Taped would be safer, but we would insist on substantial control over how my responses are edited. They can absolutely murder you in the tape room. I may already be dead, but I want the televised version of my demise to come off with a modicum of pride, grace, and dignity.

So here I sit in my office on Thanksgiving afternoon with the phone ringer turned off, staring through my reflection in the window. Andrew and Kayla, back from college for the holiday, wait for me at home. Trees along the mall are covered with millions of tiny white Christmas lights. The Washington Monument is sheathed in scaffolding, looking as if a kindergartner outlined blocks of it in black crayon. Near the top, two red lights alternate winks at planes that rise across the Potomac from the runways at Reagan International. The sun hangs low over Arlington, already tinting the clouds salmon and dust.

Tourist crowds are thinning. In another half hour they will be gone, leaving the mall to a cleanup crew of squirrels and pigeons, scattered joggers in flashing shoes, and a few harried bureaucrats rushing somewhere important. Then I will slip out through the garage downstairs and treat myself to a peaceful stroll. This time I will stop near our monument, halfway down the slope off the northwest corner. I will spread my coat on the cold dry grass and lie back. For five minutes, no more, I will gaze at the cloud and contrail tapestry drifting overhead, and when that time is up, I will brush myself off and move on.

Be well, dear Pooh—

Claire

Stainless

Even though the twelve-piece stainless cookware set was a wedding gift from Warren's parents, it is Annie's view that the set belongs in her split of things. She imagines him eating meals in restaurants from now on.

She has second thoughts after packing the set, each piece wrapped in newsprint. She takes the saucepan out, sets it on the kitchen table for him. After all, Warren does heat canned soup sometimes or beans on the stove. He'll need a pan. He's completely paranoid about aluminum and no-stick coatings, worries about all those ions and free radicals leaching into hot food. Stainless alloys are noble, he says. Inert. It's what they use, he says, in surgical implants, satellite electronics, and ocean weather buoys. Warren's head is full of facts like that, useless things he reads and remembers, arcane tidbits brought out to impress someone. In the beginning, they'd impressed her, too.

Had her husband ever cooked, she wonders, really cooked on a stove one time in their nine years of on-and-off marriage? He had not. That chore always fell to her. Always. Oh, he did cook over campfires on their few weekend hikes. And he cooked on the grill out back, of course, if you consider the damage he did to steaks "cooking." Never real range-top cooking, though. Not her Warren.

"This cookware is much too good for campfires," she says aloud, testing the sound of the words in air. Yes. She'll say it just that way when he comes back. He's taken their adopted greyhound, Marty, for a walk down by the river, trying to calm the dog. Starlings, huge flocks, have started to gather for the night. They roost in the trees that surround the house. It's not even dusk yet outside, and every branch is heavy with birds, the sky noisy with their thousand conversations. She hears them out there, more arriving every minute.

Annie digs out the lid that fits the saucepan and sets that aside for Warren, too. As she does, she realizes that'll leave her with no cover for her double boiler. Jamie bent that one while they had him, banged it on the rock garden steps outside, delighted by the noise it made. Warren promised he'd bend the rim back in shape so it'd fit again. He tried the bench vise, blunt-nosed pliers, clamped by channel-locks against shaped wood blocks. None of it worked, though. Three weeks ago she'd ordered a replacement lid from the manufacturer. They'd be gone from here before it arrived.

She is sure she can get along without it. It's been years since she used the double boiler, since she last made fudge. Thinking of it now, a craving fills her, a lust for dark fudge, a dollop to lick from a spoon. Her mouth waters, yearning for a taste. It occurs to her that Warren won't really need a lid. He'll just be heating food from a can.

Annie slides the saucepan lid off the table, intending to repack it in her kitchen box. As she does, the thing rings like a steel bell, a bright pure sound, that sound so delightful to Jamie. Annie angles the lid, twirls it by the black plastic knob, the rim like a tilted carnival ride. Her reflection flashes by. The way she looks stops her. Her lips and mouth hang slack. Her nose is blunt, a pig's snout surrounding the knob. Her eyes are taffy-pulled, monstrously mismatched. Her tongue comes out, waggles and curls, licks up toward the tip of her nose. She makes funhouse faces—a whole cast, all silly, scary freaks.

Outside, Marty barks. Starlings screech back their angry sound. Annie tosses the lid back on the kitchen table where it lands with a clang. Let the bastard have it.

Moving so far from town had been her idea. Building this house had been his. He called it their cabin in the woods. She knows what it really is—a custom log home with cathedral ceilings, ten-inch round logs with microbead foam urethane chinking. His forty-minute commute to the college, her thirty-minute drive to work, these were all part of the bargain, the plan, trying to build a place, a situation, where this marriage might actually work, trying one last time for that sweet dream.

It was doomed all along. Annie can see that now. Warren has one foot always mired in their past. If her therapist treated him instead of her, she'd tell him to calmly confront his old business, to move steadily toward resolution, to accept his powerlessness over some life events. That's how she got through the Jamie business. Get involved in the "momentness" of the day, the joy. Let old shit go. How many times had Annie tried to tell him this? Warren never listened, though, called it denial. Who was she, after all? Just someone ranting, a woman, not one of his precious books.

"Marty's wired," Warren says, coming in the door. "Those birds have him spooked." He takes off his jacket and hangs it on the doorknob.

"Wipe your feet," she says. "You'll track in starling shit."

He slips off his shoes. "They're grackles," he says, setting the shoes outside the door. "Some starlings, too. The breeds share feeding territories, and they'll roost together. More grackles out there now, though. Twice as many, I'd say."

"Ah," she says. "It's grackle shit then? How could I not know?"

"I'm just saying the flock is still growing. I'll put Marty in the garage again tonight."

"That dog," she says, "was a mistake." She cuts it off there, doesn't say what comes next.

He walks past her, his stale breeze like an invisible slap. "Hindsight," he says, as if that answers everything. And he shrugs. It's a gesture that irritates her, this shrugging of his, like an easy escape. Even in stocking feet, Warren shuffles when he walks, shuffles as if wearing loose slippers. He goes into the bedroom, where he's been filling boxes, getting his stuff ready to go.

She follows and stands in the doorway. "Marty hates being in the garage," she says. "I don't sleep, hearing him out there, pacing all night, making noises like he's trying to talk."

"He won't settle outside with birds everywhere and shotguns going off."

She walks over to him. "Let's bring Marty inside tonight," Annie says. "Here in the house. I'll fold a blanket in the corner for him, make it a treat, his last night with us."

He pulls a drawer from the bureau and drops it heavily on the bed. She can tell he's thinking. "I suppose," he says, "there's no harm in that." He grabs handfuls of underwear and stacks them in the box.

She should be filling boxes, too. The realtor said the place needed to be "decluttered." No pets. Lived in, but sparsely so. She'd be bringing buyers around tomorrow, potential buyers, after lunch. The birds should have flown off by then, off to wherever they go every day to feed. At least that part was working in their favor. Annie grabs a box and opens her closet door. "I'll hose down the steps in the morning," she tells Warren, "the patio, the flagstones in the yard."

"You sure? I can," he offers.

Annie nods. "You just take care of Marty and haul boxes." As she takes her high leather boots from the closet, an orange plastic ball rolls out, comes loopy and lopsided toward her. It stops near her foot. Jamie was forever hiding them like Easter eggs and forgetting where they were. She kept thinking they'd found them all.

She looks over. Warren is busy packing. She's almost positive he didn't notice. She nudges the ball with her shoe, guides it under the bed.

She hates that Jamie's things still show up like this. The boy is gone, returned to the adoption people months ago, the arrangement never made final, things never really working out the way they'd all hoped. Everyone agreed it was best for all involved, the only practical solution, they said, to an unfortunate situation, this whole business of placement incompatibility. What more to say? The past is the past. And no, Annie tells herself, that isn't denial.

She finds herself at the window, staring out. Her silent sigh fogs a small silver circle on the glass. She wipes it with her hand and turns back to her work. She'd managed to put so much behind her, moved on in ways she doubted Warren ever would.

Outside, a blast from a shotgun sounds and then another. It's Tanner, down the road. He's in a rage again tonight, furious about the birds. Marty's barking, which had tapered off, returns full force. The hubbub of birds rises in pitch and volume.

Warren seems oblivious to it all. "Will Cass be home in the morning?" he asks. Cass is Annie's sister. "Or Gabe?"

"Just pile my boxes on their back porch," she says. "I'll scrub and polish here, vacate from the premises before noon." On the bed, she makes a pile of folded sweaters.

Warren weaves his cardboard box flaps together, locking them. "So, you'll be sleeping there?" Her sister's place, he means.

"For a few days anyway." She doesn't know beyond that.

"Empty the refrigerator in the morning," he says. "Give Cass the perishables."

"You told me." Annie says this to the sweatshirt she's folding, more than to the man who will soon be her ex-husband. Now that it's decided, it can't come too soon.

Outside, starlings and grackles are squawking again. Marty's barking is strangled by lurches against the chain. He sounds strident and strangely human now. Annie tries to ignore the noise. She pretends it's a tv playing in another room.

They pack, working around each other, the silence in the room as loud as the din in the trees. "I said that before?" Warren asks. It's been minutes. "I said to take the refrigerator food?"

"Will you just quit about the food?" she says. "Will you?"

"There's spring asparagus in the freezer," he says, and he holds his hands up. "I'm just mentioning."

Annie's brother-in-law, Gabe, is allergic. He's adamant about it not being around. She'd hate to lose it, this asparagus she froze last June with Thanksgiving in mind.

"Cook it up?" he says. "Tonight?"

"It's almost eight o'clock."

Warren looks over at the bedroom clock. It reads 7:52. He doesn't say that she's exaggerating about the time. But that's what he thought, she's sure of it, looking over that way. She's glad for a reason to get out of that room, though, to be away from him for a while, even with all this packing to do.

In the kitchen, she takes the bag of asparagus from the freezer and floats it in a bowl of hot water to thaw. As she lifts the bowl from the sink, Warren calls her. He needs strapping tape.

In the bedroom, he's got a box topped off with shoes, their dirty soles mated together. He closes the flaps and tapes them shut. Annie opens a new drawer, starts sorting through it. When she looks at him again, a plastic ball is in his hand, this one the color of lemons. He palms it, does a quick magician's flourish. "Vanish!" he says, and the ball seems to do just that. It's in his pocket now, she knows. That's one trick Jamie never did figure out.

She turns away, the ceiling light too bright now for her eyes. Something in the way he says "vanish" is meant to hurt her, she knows, that word in this house such a wounding one.

Not a minute later, as if the hurting hadn't happened, Warren says, "We should drink up the wine tonight."

Gabe won't want wine in his house either, won't want her drinking it under his roof. She'll deal with that when the time comes. Her therapist tells her not to borrow trouble from tomorrow. She's been better about that lately, dealing with just this day.

Warren calls from the kitchen, "Two bottles left, Merlot and Pinot Noir, both full." Disposing of two bottles won't be a chore. Together they've gone through that much in a night and craved more.

Tanner's shotgun blasts again, followed by the maddening racket of birds and Marty's raspy yelps. Warren brings a bottle and two glasses into the bedroom. "Merlot first," he says. His movements are smooth now. His steps have a lilt like some jaunty little dance. Warren's gait isn't shuffling now, not even close. He seems happily unfazed by the clamor outside.

He twists the corkscrew all the way in and works the gadget's levers. The cork gives a perfect, high-pitched pop coming out. He frees the cork from the tool, and, bowing from the waist, he hands it to Annie. "Madam?"

She wafts the cork beneath her nose, sniffs noisily. It's a thing they do, a silly spoof on themselves, all phony sophistication. "Satisfactory," she says, her tone proper. "Yes, this will be fine." She feels pleased now, pleased with herself and her agreeableness, pleased with him, pleased that they will be sharing wine on this last evening together. What better way to end things? It seems fitting.

An hour later, Warren has his garage tools stowed in the back of his pickup truck. Marty's bark, intermittent now, has grown hoarse. Annie turns on the yard light and looks out. The grey-hound is circling, his short chain clipped around the galvanized pole Warren installed last spring. He set it deep and plumb. It's tall enough for an adjustable basketball goal, one made for a growing boy. The day they took Jamie back, the backboard and hoop came down. Warren trucked them off amid a jumble of bright toys, more than could possibly fit in the Goodwill collection box. The pole, anchored in concrete, was not so easily disposed of, though. And there was still the newly adopted greyhound to consider, where to tie him. A chain can girdle trees.

Annie raises her glass to sip and is surprised to find it empty again. Their stemware is too dainty for wine. When she does the pouring, she uses tumblers, not large ones but ones you don't have to refill every ten minutes. She closes the front door and goes to the kitchen for a sensible glass. She feels a sort of satisfaction as she fills it with Merlot, an embracing wine. She sips and holds the wine in her mouth to savor. It's something she needs at this difficult time. Cass and Gabe will have to understand and bend their precious house rules for the short while she's there.

Warren comes in from the garage carrying a ball of twine and an empty glass. "It looks okay out there," he says. "Not too cluttered."

"They should love the place," she says, "the prospects." A kind of uneasiness rises in her chest, like something trapped.

"We did," Warren says. He extends and wiggles the glass as if it's thirsty, not him, as if he just can't take responsibility, not even for a little thirst.

Annie pours for him. There's a slight swaying to his glass, like a lake boat set adrift. Even though she's had more wine, her hand is rock-steady as she pours. It hasn't always been that way. In the beginning, she'd been the one to get loopy first.

They'd met by accident, a reception for a visiting chemist from Nigeria. She'd been someone's emergency date, filling in for her sick roommate. Warren was there because it was expected, an obligation of his scholarship. Their mutual disinterest brought them together in a quiet backwater of the event, an alcove convenient to the wine table, the blunt-haired woman pouring there. It all seemed so predestined to them back then, a miraculous gift of fate.

It didn't turn out to be, of course. Despite their best efforts—and Annie did believe that Warren had made an effort—the marriage never seemed to work. She couldn't get pregnant, couldn't bear children, natural, in vitro, whatever. He'd known that going in. It was never her secret. Never. But knowing it isn't the same as living with it, not the way she did. Warren swore he didn't hold her infertility against her, swore it every time she accused him of what she could see so plainly on his face. He would say it was okay, always okay, repeating what she knew must be a kindly lie.

"Forget something?" Warren asks. He's holding up the asparagus, the pouch saggy now and dripping water.

She hates his attitude at times like this. "You still want it?"

He shrugs again, that damn shrug of his, and says he does.

Annie opens the cookware box, takes out the sauté pan, and puts it on to heat. She pours in olive oil, adds a splash of wine from her glass. He likes her cooking. He used to tell her so all the time. She takes a few mushrooms from the refrigerator, slices them, and cuts off the ends of young asparagus spears, cutting at a long angle. With her fingers, she places the mushrooms in the pan, spreading them. The oil spits and splatters as she lays the asparagus spears in to sauté. The aroma rises. With eyes closed, she breathes it in, this taste she's always loved.

Warren has the Pinot open now. He fills her glass beside the stove. She sips, and when the asparagus is ready, she divides the spears and mushrooms between two plates. She sprinkles on Parmesan cheese, and she calls, "Ready," even though he's right beside her. She carries the plates to the table. Warren brings her wine glass and his.

"To better days," Annie says, making a toast.

Warren lifts his glass. "They don't come much worse." He takes a drink.

Marty's bark sounds painful now, but still he can't stop barking at the raucous birds, the starlings, the grackles, whatever else has joined them on the branches. "What I mean," Annie says, "is our future, that it's better for both of us."

He cuts the asparagus, stabs pieces with his fork, eats. "And Jamie?" he says.

She slams her fork down and wads her napkin. "It's our last night here, Warren. Do we have to fight?"

His eyes seem to soften. "Do you think about him?"

Another shotgun blast, and Marty tries to bark. It hurts her to hear. "Bring him in," she says, "the damn dog."

Warren lurches to his feet. His chair topples back, banging the wall. He bumps his way through the doorway and out the front door.

When Annie reaches the front door, he's already in the yard. He's got the greyhound's collar in one hand, the chain in the other. He's struggling with the latch. The dog is frantic, turned sideways and pulling, the aging bulk of him still muscular, his legs athletic. Annie hurries down the steps and out across the lawn. She grabs the collar, strokes the dog's neck trying to soothe him. Marty can't shut up. He keeps trying to bark, even with that throat.

"Got it," Warren says, and the chain falls away. Together they lead the lunging dog toward the house. They manage to horse him up the stairs, tugging his collar and using knees against his sides. The dog's nails scrape the concrete porch like a bamboo rake. She gets the door, and Warren shoves him inside.

While Annie pulls old blankets from under the guest bed, she can hear Marty. The dog is racing through the rooms, places he's never been, as if looking for something—a way out, she thinks, or maybe a way to get at the taunting birds. She piles the blankets in the kitchen. She grabs the bowl of water left over from thawing asparagus, and she puts it on the floor. Marty is there immediately, his tongue lapping water noisily. "Calm down, baby," she says. Her hand slides across his quivering flank, patting the hair smooth.

A banging sound outside startles her. It comes from the front yard, a ringing, clanging kind of noise.

Annie hurries to the front door. On the lawn, beneath the two largest trees, Warren bangs cookware together, turning slowly in his stocking feet, looking up, stumbling across the bird shit—littered lawn. The starlings and grackles answer back with their angry squawking, their black and purple indignity, iridescent and loud. He yells at the birds, yells sounds, not words. And he bangs the cookware, clanging together a large fry pan and the saucepan lid.

She's on the porch steps watching him, just watching. Another shotgun blast from Tanner's direction startles her from her trance. She goes to get Warren's shoes, thinking that's something important, that it wouldn't be so crazy if he'd only wear shoes. She sees them now, his shoes beside the door.

The cookware box is on the porch, too, open at the top of the stairs. She rummages inside and comes out with the double boiler. She's forgotten about his shoes now. She yells at the birds trying to settle on the branches above her, watches them rise, scold back at her. She can feel her fury break loose inside. She kicks off her shoes, foot-flings them off the porch, and follows them down.

Annie goes out into the yard. She bangs the double-boiler bottoms together as she goes, clanging them together like she's marching and they're cymbals. The light is dim away from the house, even with the yard light on. She can make out Warren, though, and she heads that way, out toward the road. He's banging there, slowly turning, the fry pan dented, the pan lid bent, and still he bangs and yells. As he turns, she can see his eyes, see the glistening there. She yells now, too, yells until her lungs hurt, hollers at the million starlings and grackles she can't even see, the raucous birds that will never shut up.

THE IOWA SHORT FICTION AWARD AND JOHN SIMMONS
SHORT FICTION AWARD WINNERS, 1970–2006

Donald Anderson
Fire Road
Dianne Benedict
Shiny Objects
David Borofka
Hints of His Mortality
Robert Boswell
Dancing in the Movies
Mark Brazaitis
The River of Lost Voices:
Stories from Guatemala
Jack Cady
The Burning and Other
Stories
Pat Carr
The Women in the Mirror
Kathryn Chetkovich
Friendly Fire
Cyrus Colter
The Beach Umbrella
Jennifer S. Davis
Her Kind of Want
Janet Desaulniers
What You've Been Missing
Sharon Dilworth
The Long White
Susan M. Dodd
Old Wives' Tales
Merrill Feitell
Here Beneath Low-
Flying Planes
James Fetler
Impossible Appetites
Starkey Flythe, Jr.
Lent: The Slow Fast
Sohrab Homi Fracis
Ticket to Minto: Stories
of India and America
H. E. Francis
The Itinerary of Beggars

Abby Frucht
Fruit of the Month
Tereze Glück
May You Live in
Interesting Times
Ivy Goodman
Heart Failure
Ann Harleman
Happiness
Elizabeth Harris
The Ant Generator
Ryan Harty
Bring Me Your
Saddest Arizona
Mary Hedin
Fly Away Home
Beth Helms
American Wives
Jim Henry
Thank You for Being
Concerned and Sensitive
Lisa Lenzo
Within the Lighted City
Renée Manfredi
Where Love Leaves Us
Susan Onthank Mates
The Good Doctor
John McNally
Troublemakers
Kevin Moffett
Permanent Visitors
Rod Val Moore
Igloo among Palms
Lucia Nevai
Star Game
Thisbe Nissen
Out of the Girls' Room
and into the Night
Dan O'Brien
Eminent Domain